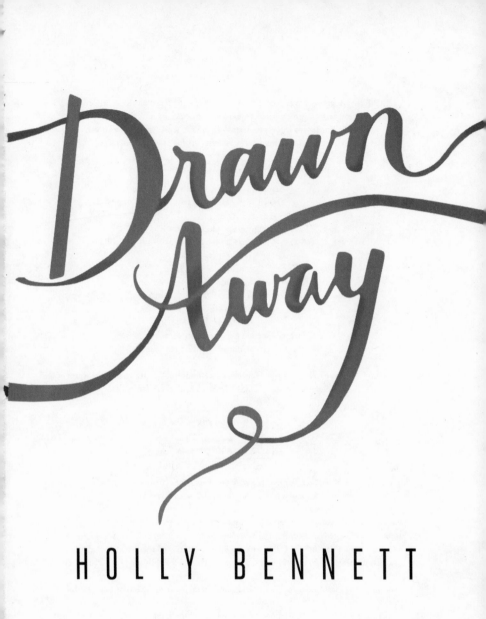

# Drawn Away

HOLLY BENNETT

ORCA BOOK PUBLISHERS

Library and Archives Canada Cataloguing in Publication

Bennett, Holly, 1957-, author
Drawn away / Holly Bennett.

Issued also in print and electronic formats.
ISBN 978-1-4598-1252-9 (hardback). —ISBN 978-1-4598-1253-6 (pdf). —
ISBN 978-1-4598-1254-3 (epub)

I. Title.
PS8603.E5595D73.2017          JC813'.6          C2016-904445-9
C2016-904446-7

First published in the United States, 2017
Library of Congress Control Number: 2016949061

**Summary**: In this paranormal novel for teens, Jack finds himself drawn into the world of
a character from one of Hans Christian Andersen's fairy tales.

*Orca Book Publishers is dedicated to preserving the environment and has
printed this book on Forest Stewardship Council® certified paper.*

Orca Book Publishers gratefully acknowledges the support for its publishing
programs provided by the following agencies: the Government of Canada through the
Canada Book Fund and the Canada Council for the Arts, and the Province of British
Columbia through the BC Arts Council and the Book Publishing Tax Credit.

Cover image by iStock.com and Shari Nakagawa. Hand lettering by Kristi-Lea Abramson
Design by Teresa Bubela
Author photo by Jordan Lyall Photography

ORCA BOOK PUBLISHERS
www.orcabook.com

Printed and bound in Canada.

20  19  18  17  •  4  3  2  1

*To my youngest son, Aaron, with thanks and admiration (not to mention love!)*

# ONE

## JACK

*The street is completely deserted, except for the girl. And it's dark, darker than it should be given the light that remains in the sky. Everything is gray and brown, as though the buildings, the cobblestones, the air itself have been tinged with soot.*

*I don't know where I am or how I got here. Strangely, I am not terrified by this fact. I gaze down the street with a kind of calm curiosity, like you do sometimes in dreams. I am dreaming, I guess, but I know it's a dream.*

*It's hard to tell how long the street is. It fades away into shadow and mist when I try to see the end. I have a sudden conviction that there is nothing beyond the mist, just as I am somehow sure that there are no people behind the grimy windows of the buildings.*

*Hard to tell how old the girl is from here. She's small, her little stick legs poking out of a bulky skirt.*

*I nearly jump out of my skin when she calls out. Her voice shatters the still air, and I realize how utterly silent it's been until now.*

*"Matches…who'll buy my matches?" It's a quavery reed of a voice, but it carries through the silence.*

*I hitch a breath and walk toward her. Even in my Nikes I can hear every footstep.*

*"Matches…who'll—oh!"*

*She stares at me like she's, well, seen a ghost. Wide blue eyes too big for her pinched little face. Scrawny shoulders hunched under a thin shawl tied in the front. She's small, all right, but maybe not as young as I thought. There's a hint of breast swelling against the press of the shawl.*

*I'm embarrassed to have noticed this and wrench my eyes away. She's looking at me kind of wildly, like the last thing she expected was an actual customer. Still, she squares her shoulders and asks, "Matches, Mister?"*

*"Um, no thanks."*

*She nods, resigned, like she expected no more.*

*"What's your name?" I ask. I can't really think of any small talk that would be suitable—Come here often? Where the hell are we?*

*"I'm the match girl." She's polite but can't quite hide the "well, duh" tone.*

*"Yes, but what's your name? I'm Jack." I'm not sure if I should offer to shake hands or something. She just looks at me blankly with those big eyes. I try again. "Where is everybody?"*

*Her thin shoulders lift in the sketchy suggestion of a shrug.*

"Gone. Everyone's gone. There's only me left." A puzzled glance. "And you."

"Where did they go?" I ask.

Again the vague shrug. Then her gaze strays to the nearest alleyway. I can't really see into it because of the gray light and the mist seeping out of its entrance. She sidles toward me. "I think it's the mist," she whispers. "It swallowed them up."

I want to tell her that's ridiculous, that mist doesn't eat people, but I look again at the mouth of the alleyway—the mouth of the alleyway—and I can't suppress the shudder that runs up my back. I glance away quickly so that it doesn't— what? Notice me? There's just something damn spooky about the way that mist oozes out and creeps along the pavement.

A sound snags my ears—very faint, but in the silence of this street I can hear it clearly enough. It's music, music being played somewhere far away...

---

The opening notes of "Für Elise" rang out in the quiet classroom, a tinny, electronic ringtone that would send Beethoven into despair. I don't know why I never reprogrammed the damn thing. It just always seemed like more trouble than it was worth. I made a quick check of my pump—*low cartridge*—and turned off the alarm.

I looked around, so disoriented I wasn't sure where I was. That dream or hallucination or whatever it was had been so real, it was still alive inside me as I tried to catch my bearings. Math class. Did I remember being in math class? My textbook was open in front of me, a half-finished problem written out on graph paper: $x$ and $y$ axes waiting to be plotted. A quiz—great. Who knew how long I'd been wigging out while the clock ticked?

Only then did it hit me. Shit. I had to be low—so low I was in la-la land. I shoved my hand into my jeans pocket and hauled out my glucose meter.

"Hand it over."

I looked up, and the teacher—Ms. Pritchard, older and no-nonsense in dress and manner—was standing beside me with her hand out.

"Sorry, what?"

"Cell phones are to be turned off during class. I was very clear about that, and the consequence. You can pick it up at the end of the period."

I was so not in the mood. "It's not a cell phone. It's the alarm on my insulin pump." I flipped up the edge of my T-shirt so she could see the tubing that ran from the pump to the infusion set stuck in my skin.

She looked as flustered as if I'd flashed her. I almost felt sorry for her, but not very. I don't care if people know I'm diabetic, and I don't do anything to hide it, but that doesn't mean I wanted to announce it to the class on my second day at a new school. Plus, I needed to test my blood sugar. Now.

"Oh. I see," she said. She took a step back as I lanced my finger and squeezed out more blood than was strictly necessary. "Well, um, anything you need to do about that, you go ahead."

"That's okay, it will wait until after class," I said as she beat a retreat back to her desk. Amazingly, it was true. My reading was 6.5, damn near perfect for three hours past breakfast—but if I wasn't low, what the hell had just happened to me?

I tried to focus on the quiz, but I knew my results wouldn't be great. I couldn't stop thinking about that girl, and the silence…and the mist. I wasn't worried about the math—it was just a little beginning-of-year diagnostic—but I was pretty freaked out about the other thing. What if I had a brain tumor or some kind of sudden-onset psychosis? I thought about the coffee I'd bought at the caf that morning—wretched coffee, even worse than at my old school. Could someone have dropped a hit of acid in there? *Hey, big joke, let's dope up the new guy*? It seemed beyond unlikely.

The class finally ended, and as we filed out the door a girl who'd been sitting a couple of seats over caught my eye. She grimaced sympathetically. "Talk about invasion of privacy. Like the old bat would have any right to take your stuff anyway, even if it *was* a phone."

I gave a snort of laughter. It wasn't really funny, but it made me feel better, like I was back in the normal world for real—just two students, dissing their teacher.

"Yeah, well, my mom would say I should have told all my teachers about my diabetes the first day, and then crap like this wouldn't happen," I replied. "Which is true, but…"

She nodded. "Why should you have to?"

I took a more careful look at her. My old school in Montreal had attracted lots of quirky, oddball kids. She would have fit right in. Here in small-town Ontario, she stood out: choppy dyed-black hair, purple tights and black Doc Martens. She didn't look as tough as she should though—her blue eyes were too big, her frame too delicate. She was actually really little.

"I'm Jack."

"Lucy." She extended her hand with an awkward little laugh, and we did this clumsy, jokey handshake. "Welcome to Purgatory," she said. And then she headed off down the hall, leaving me to find a reasonably direct route to room 312.

## LUCY

I thought about the new boy on my walk home. It's a longish walk, but a lot of it borders the river, so in spring and fall it's nice. In the winter it can be windy as hell, and I don't even see the river because I'm bent over, trying to keep my face from freezing.

It was nearly dinnertime—I had hung out with my friend Ali for a while after school—so the sun was low, shafting out of the clouds in spears, and the light on the little hummocks and islands in the river was incredibly beautiful.

I thought about painting it, wishing I was good enough to capture light like that without it looking like some sentimental jigsaw-puzzle picture. Mist was rising off the water, which you hardly ever see at this time of day.

The new guy was cute. Not really my type—or more precisely, I didn't suppose I was *his* type—but cute. Nice open smile. Clean-cut though. Probably destined for some blond athletic girl with her boobs spilling out the top of her push-up bra.

I gave myself a mental smack for that last bit. Where do thoughts like that come from? I'd been on the receiving end of plenty of catty remarks, and I did not want to play that game, not even in my own mind.

I was cutting through the park when it started to rain a bit, just a fine drizzle that turned the air silvery. I hunched my head down the way you do at first with rain, even though it's pointless. So I didn't notice the girl floating over the river until I was almost directly across from her—and then I stopped in my tracks.

She was faint, like she was half made of mist herself, but she was definitely not a girl-shaped cloud. I was staring at a skinny waif with old-fashioned clothes and hollow cheeks and wide blue eyes; she was just standing there, her feet swathed in mist and the river running beneath her.

Suddenly spiders were crawling up the back of my neck. My first impulse was to turn around, run back to the road and pretend it never happened. But I couldn't make my feet move, and even if I could have—well, she was too amazing. My mind was already fighting back the spiders, too curious to run. *What was she?*

I thought back to tenth grade, two years ago—AKA The Year I Messed Up—and wondered uneasily if some drug or other was coming back to haunt me. But that didn't make sense, not really. I never had hallucinations or whatever, not even in the thick of it.

She turned—or more like *drifted*—around so she was directly facing me, but she didn't seem to see me. Her mouth was moving. I stared at her, trying to lip-read, and oh God, then I could hear her. Her thin little voice was right inside my head, and the spiders were all over me, scuttling around like mad things.

She just repeated one name, over and over.

"Jack?" She stared out with her empty, lost eyes. "Jack?"

And that's when I started running.

~⌇~

My mom was at work when I got home, and for once I actually locked the door behind me like she was always nagging me to. I just stood there with my back to the door, panting and waiting for my heart to slow down. Once my legs had unlocked in the park, I'd run pretty much the whole way home—and trust me, I'm not a runner. Now they wanted to collapse under me, but it seemed important to stay upright, like somehow that would help me keep a grip on reality.

I saw some weird stuff when I was AWOL, but there was nothing in my experience to explain a random sighting of a floating girl. I didn't know how to deal with her, so I made tea and ate half a tub of ice cream instead, wondering if maybe I should go back for more sessions with my therapist, Kate.

A flare of the old anger at my mom licked up. I knew she had to work, and I knew she still slept badly and preferred the evening shift so she didn't have to get up at the crack of dawn. I'm not even sure I would have told her what happened if she *had* come home for dinner. It's just, you know, sometimes it would be nice to have some company. No, that's a half-truth. What I really mean is, sometimes I miss having her fuss over me like she used to. Make a nice meal for us to share, ask how my day went, admire my drawings, whatever. Ask annoying questions about where I'm going and when I'm getting home. Be a mom.

Kate said everyone grieves on their own timetable, in their own way. Fair enough. I didn't exactly handle Dad's death well myself. But I couldn't help thinking I might have done better if she hadn't been so…gone.

I knew there was leftover quiche in the fridge, so I didn't need to think about dinner. I put on Tacocat—count on girl surf punk to blow away the cobwebs and fortify your soul—and cranked it up till the bass boomed in my chest. Then I pulled out my sketch pad. Maybe if I put her on paper, I could get that little girl out of my head.

# TWO

## KLARA

I know I'm dead. Of course I do. I was a little confused at first, but I figured it out soon enough. Perhaps it was when I noticed I wasn't hungry. I was hungry most of my life, but I am never hungry or cold or sick now. I don't feel full or warm or well either—I don't feel anything at all.

It was strange how it happened. I rarely sold many matches, but that day it was like I was invisible. And it's true I was scared to go home, if you can call it home. My father had promised to beat me bloody if I returned with empty pockets again. So I thought I would just stay where I was until I either sold something or it was late enough that he'd be passed out from drink, and I could sneak onto the pile of rags he called a bed and at least be out of the wind, if not warm. I didn't think I'd ever be warm again.

But it got later and later, and the street emptied of people, everyone rushing home to their fires, and I kept putting off going home. It's like I was too tired and cold to summon up the effort. I kept thinking, Soon I'll get started, and then some while later I would realize that I was still standing there, all alone on a dark street. My mind started wandering, and at some point I looked up and found I was crouched in the little corner formed by the wall of a building and its brick entranceway. Sometime later my head snapped up and I realized I'd actually been sleeping. By then I couldn't feel my feet or my hands, which was a blessing because until then they had been a torment. I remember thinking lazily, it will be morning soon—I might best stay where I am.

And that's where I was found, dead as a doorpost, the next morning. I stood there and watched two men throw the pale, stiff body into a cart, like so much rubbish, and I didn't realize for some time that it was my body they were hauling away.

At first the street seemed much as it always had, except that nobody noticed me. But then, they never had taken much notice of me, so that wasn't much different either. Then the mist began moving in, filling in the alleyways, seeping out from under the doors. And little by little, so that I hardly noticed at first, the people thinned out. It went from a bustling street to a quiet street to an empty street.

I hadn't seen another soul in the longest time when that boy appeared. Outlandish thing he was, with his strange clothes, but so clean and healthy-looking.

Teeth that would blind you, they were so white and even. *"What's your name?"* he asked me. And it made me wonder—I must have had a name once. My father never used it; he just called me "girl," or worse. But when I was a baby, when my mother was still with us, she must have given me a name.

Jack. His name was Jack. He arrived out of nowhere and disappeared just as suddenly. But he saw me! And he left me full of questions that have never occurred to me, like my name. And this one: why am I here? I told Jack I thought the mist had eaten the other people, and that is how it had seemed to me. But now I wonder if all those people just…moved on, and I am the one who is stuck. If I stayed too long after I died, and now I can't leave. It never occurred to me to try until now. But I can't. I am just here, selling matches to nobody.

I wonder if that boy Jack will come back. I hope he does. I didn't talk to him properly last time. He took me by surprise, and I'm not used to talking to people. But I would like to, maybe.

Come back, Jack.

Come back.

# THREE

## JACK

I headed straight to the bus after school so I could grab an empty seat before it filled up. I settled in with some tunes (the armor of awkward new kids). My knee drummed along with We Are Wolves, but I wasn't really listening. I was trying to think about what had happened in math class. Problem was, who knows *how* to think about a thing like that?

A body dropped into the seat beside me, and I glanced up with a neutral smile, then relaxed as I recognized a guy from drama class—Ryan? Rick?

"Jack, right?"

I nodded and slipped out the earbuds. "I'm gapping out on your name, man, but I do remember you like lynxes." Only in drama class would this be one of the first things you learned about a seventeen-year-old guy—but then, only in drama would you feel like you knew anything about a person after only two classes.

"Rafe. And honestly, I pretty much just pulled a lynx out of the air."

"I wasn't too thrilled with my own choice." I should have anticipated that after the easy icebreaker of *name an animal you'd like to be*, the next step would be to act it out. And there I was, a croaking, flapping raven. It could have been worse though; one poor girl had said *armadillo*.

"It'll be a good class though, I think."

I thought so too. I discovered a love of acting in tenth grade, when a timetable conflict landed me with a choice of drama, Spanish or creative writing. I figured drama would be the easiest—and maybe it was—but it also turned out to be fun. It's a different kind of challenge, you know? After my first play—in which I had a bit part and built sets—I was hooked.

"So where're you from?"

And suddenly my social life was looking a whole lot brighter. By the time my stop came up, I'd thumbed through Rafe's mind-bogglingly massive music collection, and he'd invited me to come along to a show at a local club on Friday night.

And I hadn't thought once about the weird little Match Girl.

---

The house was empty when I got home; I get off school a bit earlier than my brother, who's in his last year of elementary. I headed for the kitchen. I hadn't felt much like eating at lunchtime—between the awkwardness of having no one to eat with and the weirdness of my math class episode, my stomach had been a little tense—but I was starving now.

I was most of the way through a bowl of mac and cheese when Noah got home.

"Mac and cheese on the stove if you want it," I said.

"Sweet." Noah loaded up a bowl and sprawled at the table. "I thought Mom said she wasn't going to buy this crap anymore."

I grinned. "Dad and I did the shopping last time, remember?"

I let Noah eat for a while before asking, "So how are things going at school so far?"

Noah hunched his shoulders in annoyance. "Fine, Mom."

"C'mon."

The move, my parents had admitted, was badly timed for both of us. It sucked that after graduating (high school ends with eleventh grade in Quebec), I now had to go *back* to high school for twelfth grade in Ontario. Going from an alternative school to a regular school just added insult to injury. But at least for me, it would only be one year, and then I'd be done. Noah was in eighth grade; he was going to spend his whole teenagerhood here.

Noah shoveled in a large mouthful of mac and cheese and chewed down the bulk of it before replying.

"Nobody's tried to beat me up. And nobody's asked me to be their best friend either. It's day two—what do you expect?"

"Fair point," I said. "That's about where I'm at too. I met a cute girl though."

*Cute* wasn't at all the right word for Lucy. But she was…*something*. I hoped I could talk to her again soon, more than just a few words in the hallway.

⁓

I intended to tell my parents about what had happened that morning, I really did. When you're diabetic from the age of twelve, you get used to your parents knowing more about your life than most teenagers would prefer. We had a pact that I would tell my parents if I was drinking and come home rather than stay at a friend's, so they could test me in the night and help me stay safe. And I actually did, though every instinct in my body told me to stay under the radar and keep my first beers a secret.

I thought I could tell my dad about my weird vision without him freaking out. Mom would drag me into the hospital emergency room and demand a CAT scan right away. Dad would be more likely to say something like, *Probably just a really vivid daydream. Still, maybe we should check it out with the doctor, just to be sure.* That's what I wanted to hear.

So I waited through dinner, only half hearing my parents' conversation. Of course, when I tested before eating, I was high from the mac and cheese. When I keyed in the correction dose on my pump, I could almost see my mom clamp her lips together to keep herself from asking about my meter reading. She's supposed to be backing off, letting me deal with it on my own—given that I'll probably be living away from home next year—but it's hard for her.

"Hey, I think I found a good space to hold my prenatal classes," she announced brightly, determinedly not watching while I piled food on my plate, figured out the carb count and added that to my already hefty dose of insulin. "There's a sort of community center with nice comfy rooms they rent out, very reasonable."

"That's great," Dad said. "Do you think you'll get enough people?"

Mom sighed. "Remains to be seen. People think they can learn everything from the Internet now." Mom had worked in Montreal as a doula and prenatal teacher, helping women give birth, so she was starting over just like us.

Dad started talking about this provincial park he had learned about from some guy at work. "Only an hour's drive away! And no motorboats at all allowed—can you imagine how quiet?" This is what we came here for, I guess. Dad's a fish biologist, and this new job with the Ministry of Natural Resources is better than his old one. But also, as my mom pointed out, he became a fish biologist because he loves being on lakes and rivers and in the bush—he's not really a city guy. So, unlike my brother and me, he loved the idea of moving to a smaller city surrounded by waterways.

I get it, I really do. I actually like outdoor stuff a lot too. But I was missing my friends and the action and Montreal itself—the bagel shop on the corner with the big wood oven, the sound of French everywhere, the pretty people strutting their stuff down St. Denis, the grittiness of the Metro. I even missed the slight tension of summoning up my French to order lunch or whatever.

Now it was our turn, and of course my mom asked how we were doing with school, and Noah and I both served up the automatic "fine." Mom looked pained, so I volunteered that my drama class seemed good and I had met a cool guy on the bus, and that earned a relieved smile. But it also put more pressure on Noah to come up with something, so he retaliated with "Jack also met a cute *girl*."

A masterful deflection.

Noah needed a bunch of things for school, so after dinner Mom took him out shopping. This was my chance to talk to Dad, but before I could say anything he rubbed his hand over his face and said, "Would you mind doing the dishes tonight, Jack? I didn't sleep for shit last night and could really use a lie-down."

So I did, and then Mom and Noah were back and everyone was downstairs watching TV, and the longer

I waited, the harder it was to even remember what exactly had happened in math class.

~ㅇㅇ~

The next morning I walked into the kitchen in time to witness a spectacular kitchen malfunction involving my dad, a stubbed toe and a full pot of coffee. We were all delayed, and I had to scramble for the bus. By the time I got home, the weird little Match Girl didn't seem nearly so real, and I managed to convince myself that I'd just nodded off and had a dream or something. Anyway, I had more important things to think about—like getting a life in this new town.

## LUCY

The day after I saw the floating girl, I finally got a guidance appointment to fix my timetable. Somebody must have miscopied the course code or something; in any case, I'd ended up in data management instead of drama. That, for me, is a very bad substitution. I was afraid that drama would already be filled or that it would take too much rearranging to make it work, but in the end I only had to switch English classes to make it all fit.

Another nice surprise: I walked into drama with my transfer slip, and who should I see there but Jack.

His face lit up like he was really glad to see me, and I couldn't help but smile back. He does have a very nice smile.

We ended up in the same group, reading and blocking out a scene from *Twelfth Night*. Jack's a good reader, managing to get the sense of the dialogue and not just spit out the words. I'm more interested in set and costume design than acting, but I like to think I held my own.

On Friday Ali and I went to the Ruby Room for an all-ages concert, and there was Jack, paying his cover charge and getting the hand stamp that proclaimed him underage. He was there with Rafe and some of his friends. That's good—Rafe's a sweet guy, and he hangs with nice people. Jack and I danced a bit and hung out on the sidewalk between sets to cool off, and by the time Ali's parents came to pick us up, he had suggested we partner up on our math homework this year.

"I'm so in," I agreed. I'm okay at math but not at all interested in it, so from both an efficiency and a diversionary perspective, it was a no-brainer.

We started our math club that week. I rode home with him on the bus, ignoring the incredulous look Becky Silverman shot my way and trying not to read the thought bubble over her head: *Ugh, what's he doing with* her? Obviously I failed, but I've learned not to care—much. The Becky Silverman Seal of Approval is not high on my wish list.

Jack lived in one of the tall old two-and-a-half-story houses common in Kershaw, with a bay window, an overgrown front garden and a big porch with vines screening the west side. He took one look at the cars parked out front and hauled me around to the back door.

"My mom's a La Leche League leader," he explained as he fiddled with the lock. "This many cars out front means there are probably six women inside all nursing their babies and talking about latching and milk supply and plugged ducts."

He flashed me a grin. "It would likely be less embarrassing for you than it was for my ninth-grade buddies, but still. My mom used to collar us and make me introduce them. She thinks it's good for kids to be exposed to the Wholesome Goodness of Breastfeeding. Isaac Boseley wouldn't go in my house for three years unless I went ahead and gave the all-clear."

A hoot of laughter escaped me, and I stifled it quickly—we were in the kitchen by then, and I wasn't sure I wanted to call attention to my presence. Jack was in the fridge, rooting around. "You hungry? Let's see...ham sandwich?" He opened a pantry cupboard. "Granola bars? Oh—yes—brownies!"

"Brownies sound good," I said.

"What do you want to drink? Tea, juice? Or I can make you an espresso."

Oh my. I liked Jack's house already.

~⁊~

I sipped at the strong, rich coffee and watched Jack demolish a sandwich, a glass of milk and a brownie.

"Didn't you have lunch?" I teased.

"I'm a growing boy," he said. "This is second lunch."

Before he ate, he pulled out the gadgets I had seen him use in math class. One was a little bigger than a USB stick. He pressed it against his fingertip and brought out a drop of blood. Then he held his finger against a strip inserted into the second gadget. There was a beep, he checked the readout, and then he pushed some buttons on what looked like a pager clipped at his waistband.

"So what is all that stuff?" I asked. Then I regretted it. Wasn't our very first conversation about how he shouldn't have to explain it to people? But he didn't seem to mind.

"This meter," he said, showing me the little thingy he'd put the strip into, "measures my blood sugar. I need to know that to figure out the right amount of insulin to take. The pump gives it to me." Somehow half the sandwich disappeared during those sentences.

"How often do you have to prick your finger like that?"

"A lot. When I get up, when I go to bed, when I eat. Then, let's see, when I drive, when I exercise, when I'm sick, when I party, when the moon aligns with Mars…it adds up."

I remember getting my thumb stabbed to get my blood typed before I had my adenoids out. Granted, I was little, but it hurt like crazy. Jack didn't seem to even notice it. "Does it hurt?" I blurted out. God, probably every bozo he met asked him that.

"Hardly at all. Want to try it?" The challenge in his voice was not obvious, but it was there. I bet nobody ever tried it.

I had a tattoo, for God's sake. I could do a finger prick. "Sure, okay. I mean...is it safe?" Jack looked healthy enough, but shared needles and all that.

"Yeah, totally. I just have to put in a new lancet—it's sterile."

I held out my finger, and there was a fleeting prick. Then Jack held my finger against a little strip on his meter. When it beeped, he checked the screen.

"What's it say?"

"Four point nine. You're good." That grin again. "So now...time for some math?"


## JACK

I was a bit relieved to find out Lucy's decent at math. I mean, she seems cool, and I did suggest we buddy up partly so I could hang out with her. But it occurred to me when I was walking home on Friday night that I could have unwittingly volunteered to be a math tutor—not exactly what I had in mind.

We were working at the kitchen table when Noah got home. He grunted hello, grabbed a brownie and headed down to the rec room.

"What's down there?" Lucy asked.

"TV, video games, computer—all the bad stuff."
A volley of delighted, high-pitched yips floated up the
stairs. "Oh, and our puppy, Snowball. Mom crates him
when she's having meetings if there's no one home to keep
an eye on him."

Lucy perked up. "Can we go down and meet him
when we're done?"

"Yeah, of course."

Snowball is the wiggly little armful of black fuzz my
parents got as a moving bribe for Noah. We'd begged peri-
odically for a dog in Montreal, but my dad didn't believe
city life was good for dogs, and my mom didn't like the
thought of having to bundle up for a walk every time the
dog had to pee. Our new house has a fenced backyard that
made it possible to have Snowball.

Noah had given Lucy a wide berth in the kitchen,
but when she plopped down beside him on the floor,
Snowball barreled into her arms. He licked her face
maniacally, and she just giggled and let him. Then she
rolled him on his back and rubbed his belly until he
melted into an ecstatic puddle.

"So who named him Snowball?"

"I did," Noah admitted.

"It's perfect." Noah flashed her a grateful smile, and I
could see him relax. He's intimidated by older girls, under-
standably, and Lucy—well, with the boots and hair, she
looks intimidating at first. But she put him right at ease.

"So you like animals?" Noah asked.

"Love them," she replied. "All kinds."

Another smile, evil this time. "Jack has pets too."

"Show!" she demanded. Then she caught the look I shot Noah. "Wait, what are they—tarantulas or something?"

"Go show her, Jack."

~ ⁊ ~

We stepped into my room, and Lucy's eyes fastened on the big cage on the dresser. I made a chirpy noise, and suddenly the bedding rustled and two little heads popped up. Then the girls climbed up the cage bars and clung there staring at me, hoping for a treat or some action.

Lucy took in the beady black eyes, the long scaly tales hanging down. "Are those *rats*?" she squealed.

Disappointing—I wouldn't have pegged her for a squealer. I launched into my spiel. "Yeah, but honestly they're really—"

"I've always wanted a rat!"

End of spiel. I'm pretty sure I've never heard anyone say that before.

"Really?"

"I campaigned hard for one when I was nine or ten. I had this book from the library that talked about what great pets they were, but my mom just couldn't get her head around it. She wasn't trying to be mean, she just… they give her the creeps."

"Her and a lot of other people."

I opened the door of the cage and the rats jostled through, each trying to run out first.

I turned to Lucy with my hands full of rat. She was grinning from ear to ear. "The black-and-white one is Popcorn, and the gray one is Pip. Hold out your hands."

They went right to her, curious as always. Pip climbed up her sleeve to perch on her shoulder. Popcorn found Lucy's front hoodie pocket, dove in and then poked her head out.

"Should I rescue you?" I asked.

Lucy giggled as Pip began checking out her earrings. "No way."

I had a good feeling about this girl.

# FOUR

## KLARA

I haven't seen that boy Jack in a long time. I think about him though. I think about him a good deal.

I can't recall what I thought about before he came. I don't believe I thought anything at all. It's as though he woke me up, and now I want to stay awake.

I try to remember exactly what he looked like. I start at his head and move down. If I can imagine him perfectly, in every detail, it will be like he's standing here before me.

His hair is outlandishly short—close to his head all over—and dark brown. He wears no hat. You would think he must be terribly poor, not to have a hat, but he doesn't look poor. He's tall and straight, with wide shoulders and clear eyes and those lovely teeth. I'll wager he never had a toothache in his life.

Another odd thing: his skin has turned brown from the sun, like a farmer's, but his hands are smooth, the nails clean and even. A gentleman's hands. But I've run ahead. I'm not even at his neck yet!

His clothing was so strange. No jacket, no waist-coat, just a plain, close-cut, short tunic that left his arms almost entirely bare. Some soft, thin fabric I've never seen, and the color! A deep royal blue that only a rich man, surely, could afford.

When I'm not remembering Jack, I'm remembering my life. I'd rather not, truly, but it comes to me now unbidden. The cold, the hunger, the beatings, my father's brute drunken ravings. I felt safer on the street corner than in my own home—but even that was changing, wasn't it, as I got older? How many men, that last year, came leering up to me? *"I don't need no matches, Missy, but I'll pay you a mark to have a go in that alleyway with me!"* I had to run off more than once, when they wouldn't take no for an answer.

And that last night. It wasn't just a beating my father had threatened. His shouts echoed down the street after me. *"You've bled me dry since the day you were born, but by God, girl, you'll earn your keep now! I don't care how you get it, but you come back here with some real money! Real money, mind, or after I knock the stuffing out of you I'll sell you to the first fancy man who'll take you!"*

I hated him by then. I never disobeyed him, never did anything but his bidding, but I only got cuffs and curses back.

Was my mother different, when she lived? Did she hold me and feed me and warm me at night? A memory of her seems to hover in the air before me, just out of reach, the sound of her voice in my ears.

It's just a foolish wish, nothing more. My mother abandoned me, as my father reminded me often enough. I don't want these memories. Jack made me think of them, and now I can't stop.

I'll think about Jack again. His arms look strong— I could see the swell of his muscles—but lean. He wears something around his wrist—a sort of bracelet, with silver on it.

Come back, Jack. Come back and talk to me again.

# FIVE

## JACK

"So, *mon gars*, when are you coming back to civilization for a visit?"

It was a common refrain with my friends from Montreal. Or things like, *How are you surviving in Tim Hortonsland?* and *How's your mullet coming along?*

It was nearly the end of September, and I was Skyping with my friend, Michel. I found myself saying, "Thanksgiving, I hope. Can't wait to see you guys. But really, Michel, it's not bad here."

My reaction to Michel's snotty little crack made me realize I was already starting to feel comfortable here. I mean, Kershaw was definitely small, but I was discovering there were nice things about that—like how easy it was to find your friends downtown. The fact I already had some to meet was the nicest surprise. I'd always gotten along easily with people, but I wasn't sure I'd find "real" friends here, if that makes sense. Okay, to be honest, I was worried they might all be lame hicks. That thought seemed pretty ignorant now. My new school had its share of jerks—they all do—but Rafe was great, and he'd introduced me to a group of kids I already liked.

Even the school itself was not so bad. At my old school, they were always talking about "lifelong learning" and "self-direction." That meant we were given a lot of responsibility for our own work: *What interests you in this course? What are your learning goals? How will you demonstrate you've achieved them?* In a way it was good, but, like anything that's repeated too often, it got to be a tedious pain in the butt, and we mostly bullshitted our way through it. Still, the regimentation of my new school had rubbed me the wrong way at first—until I realized how much easier it was. Show up for class, read chapter eight, do the assignment. It was kind of a relief, honestly.

And Lucy—Lucy was awesome. I'd never met a girl quite like her. She had this kick-ass sort of don't-mess-with-me look, but that's not what she was like—at least, not entirely. She was funny and smart and, I don't know, direct, but not in a rude way, just like she knew who she was and wasn't going to pretend to be anyone else. I really liked spending time with her and was already hoping we'd be a lot more than math buddies before too long.

I began to realize there were things I didn't understand about Lucy though. I noticed she didn't seem to have that many friends at school, though Rafe and his gang were happy to have her hang out with us. She was friends with this girl, Ali, who also seemed to be a bit of a loner, and a couple of others. But she didn't hesitate when I asked if she wanted to come along to a party Rafe's friend Alex was having, and she seemed to have a good time.

I asked Rafe about it a few days ago. He hesitated before he spoke.

"Lucy had kind of a bad time a while back—I guess it was near the end of ninth grade. Her dad died, and she seemed okay at first, but then…I didn't know her very well, so I don't really know what happened, and anyway I guess it's up to her to tell you if she wants to. But she disappeared for a while, and then partway through the following fall she came back, looking like she does now."

"What did she look like before?" I asked, though it was the least of my questions.

Rafe shrugged. "I dunno. More like everyone else, I guess." I pointed silently at his loud Hawaiian shirt, and he laughed. "Don't get me wrong—it's not that I think everyone *should* look like everyone else. I like Lucy, and I'm glad we're hanging out more." He shrugged again, and I could see he was baffled himself. "I think we were…well, maybe a bit scared of her when she first came back. Maybe it was just easier to stick with the friends we already had."

So overall, things were going pretty well for me. I thought maybe Noah was having a harder time of it, though he hadn't said anything. He'd been home every weekend, and that didn't seem a good sign. But I figured things would be better once hockey started up. Noah's a decent player and really loves the game—unlike my mom. She wouldn't let him try out for the triple-A team last year, saying it would eat up all of our time and money. She tries to be supportive though, despite muttering about "war games" and "sanctioned violence," and she took him to register the day after we moved in. He'd make friends on the team.

⁓

On our third math session, Mom asked Lucy to stay for dinner. Lucy kind of ducked her head and said almost formally, "Thanks, Mrs. Lavoie, I'd like to."

Mom gave this bemused laugh and said, "Oh gosh, just call me Bente."

"Bente," Lucy said. "I've never heard that name before."

"It's Danish. I have to spell it a lot."

At dinner, the Parental Interrogation began.

"So, Lucy, what do your parents do?" my dad asked.

"It's just me and my mom," Lucy replied softly. "She works at a retirement home. Three-to-eleven shift, mostly."

"Oh, is she a nurse?" Mom asked. She has a love-hate relationship with medical people, depending on their attitude toward midwives and home birth and stuff like that.

Lucy shook her head. "Admin and reception, mostly. Though I don't think much happens after nine." Thankfully, the subject of her father was left behind. Mom moved on to grilling Noah about his geography project, and Dad launched into his concerns about the coming invasion of the Asian carp—which I would normally have been interested in, actually, but that night I was distracted. I was thinking that when we were alone again, Lucy might tell me about her dad, and sure enough she did.

We were on the couch downstairs, nominally watching *Bob's Burgers*, but she was restless. Then she reached for the remote, clicked it off and turned to me.

"It's probably time I told you about my checkered past," she said. And I just shut up and let her tell it.

"My dad died when I was fifteen." It came out flat and blunt. "A car crash on the highway to Ottawa. It was— well, you can imagine. It was bad."

I nodded sympathetically, but I couldn't imagine, or maybe I didn't want to.

"My mom kind of fell apart. I mean, we were both— oh God—" She faltered. I waited. She took her hand away from the frayed cuff she'd been worrying and began again. "Of course, you fall apart. But she sort of stayed that way. It was like she just—went away. Day after day. And there I was, trying to make sure that there was food in the house and that she ate something and that the bills were paid.

"Finally, she had to do something because we were broke. There was a big mortgage and hardly any life insurance, and my mom only had a part-time job. She had to sell the house and find full-time work, and we moved into a little townhouse. We got through all that, and I did what I could to help. But that seemed to be all she could manage. I felt like she couldn't even see me."

Lucy stopped. She ruffled up and then smoothed down her choppy hair, crossed her legs and sighed. "My dad died in March. I was in ninth grade. I held it together, barely, till the end of the school year, and then—I just got really angry. At her, at everything. We had some huge screaming fights. I was acting like a complete bitch, but I think I was just trying to get *some* kind of reaction. After a couple of weeks of that, I took off. I caught a bus to Toronto and stayed in a hostel for a few days, and when my money ran out I began panhandling and sleeping in parks. I met some people, and the longer I stayed away, the harder it was to come home. I hated it, and I was scared almost all the time, but I felt like I couldn't go back."

"Your mom must have been crazy worried," I said. I tried to picture my mother as a sudden widow. She'd be heartbroken, but I was as sure as I could be that her reaction would be to grab hold of me and Noah and hang on for dear life. But maybe that's what Lucy had expected of her mom too. Who knows how something like that will affect you?

She looked at me seriously. "I guess that was the point. But I was in counseling for quite a while before I could see it. At the time, I thought she deserved it, that I was just giving her what she wanted."

"What made you come home?" I asked.

"For one thing, it was October, and it was getting damn cold." She flashed a quick, tense smile. "But more important, I had two scary things happen to me two nights in a row. A pimp with this poor girl in tow—God, she looked awful: bruises under her makeup and so stoned she could hardly keep her eyes open—tried to recruit me, and not by asking politely. And then a crackhead pulled a broken bottle on me and threatened to cut my face up if I didn't give him money. He had me up against the wall, and if one of those bike cops hadn't come pedaling by, I don't know if I would have got away. I ran until I felt like my head was going to explode, and when I stopped I was at the bus station. And I knew I had to get my life back together, or I was going to end up dead."

Wow. I felt like a ten-year-old kid, like nothing bad had ever happened to me. I didn't know what to say, so I just put my arm around her and pulled her in close, and she snuggled right up to me. She didn't cry though. She sniffed and dragged the back of her hand across her nose and dogged on through.

"So. I didn't have bus fare. I had to call my mother, and she left work and drove up and got me. She found me a counselor and I started going, and I went to the guidance office at school to figure out how to catch up." She made a face. "I couldn't quite do it, not without a round of summer school."

"And you and your mom?" I asked.

"We made peace."

I nodded cautiously. *Made peace* didn't sound exactly like what you'd hope for.

## LUCY

I'd been okay for quite a while. All last year, I was fine. I kept up in school, got my part-time barista job, cooked myself something decent to eat most nights, got along okay with my mom.

But now I was actually happy. I used to wake up in the morning and sort of gird myself for the day. Now, pretty often, I woke up looking forward to it. And that was mostly because of Jack. I was pretty messed up when I first came back to school, and I was working so hard to get my life together and get caught up that I really didn't have room for anything else. I wasn't exactly approachable, I guess. And maybe that kind of set the tone for my social life. But Jack is the kind of person who connects easily with people, and he was connecting me up too. Now everything was easier. It was like we all—

including me—had discovered that I *wasn't* prickly or antisocial or scary. At least, not anymore.

Was I falling for him? Yes, I was. And I was pretty sure he liked me too, but he was a bit hard to read. For all his easy friendships, he seemed more reserved in that department than a lot of guys.

It's funny how I assumed at first that he was too preppy and straight for me. Then I caught sight of a photo in his room—a group of kids, all hugging and mugging for the camera. Quite a motley assortment—white and brown and Asian, long hair and punk spikes, a girl with black everything, including major eyeliner, and another who looked like she'd escaped from the 1970s.

"Who're all these kids?" I asked.

"Oh, those are my friends in Montreal." He came closer to look over my shoulder.

"Really. They don't look like you."

Jack laughed. "Don't you recognize me?"

I looked again, and there he was, hair down to his shoulders, but the same megawatt smile.

"Omigod, it's you!" More laughter while I compared the before and after. "Why'd you cut it?"

He shrugged. "Sort of a rite of passage, I guess. We did it at my going-away party—the girls went at me with scissors, and then Michel pulled out his clippers. A fresh start." He ran his hand over his head. The bristly buzz cut was just beginning to soften and lie down. "I actually liked it in the hot weather, but I hope it's a fair bit longer by winter."

I looked up at him, hovering just above my shoulder, and had a sudden strong urge to lean in and kiss him. Instead, I put the photo back on his dresser and mumbled something about getting back to the books.

So I guess it wasn't just Jack who was acting reserved.

# SIX

## LUCY

Jack offered a couple of times to meet at my house, but I put him off. I wasn't ashamed of it or anything—I just liked hanging out at Jack's. Even though it was distracting, I liked the activity—his brother Noah, who's shy and sweet, and the pets and even the mommy groups that were sometimes camped in the living room.

My house—well, it didn't feel like home, not yet anyway. It was as if there was something we'd never got around to unpacking when we moved here two years ago—the thing that makes a house feel comfy and welcoming.

So we were at Jack's again, and neither of us felt like working. It was a perfect early-October day, a sky so clear and blue that it hurt to look at it. We played with Snowball in the backyard, chasing him through the first scattering of fallen leaves and wrestling with him, and then we flopped down against the trunk of the big maple tree and admired the way the sun slanted through the yellow leaves and turned them into something glowing and magical.

And then Jack leaned over and kissed me. It was just a little brush on the corner of my mouth that left me room to call it a friendship kiss or even ignore it if I wanted to. But I didn't. I looked over and he was watching me, waiting. I smiled and tipped my face up, and we kissed again, properly, and this ridiculous wave of happiness washed through me. Relief too, because I'd known already that I had a thing for Jack—but what if he didn't for me?

We kissed gently at first, getting a feel for each other, and then the heat ramped up and the world faded away and I felt like I could make out with Jack here in the golden light forever. I wished he still had his long hair so I could reach up and grab a handful. Jack pulled me closer, and we wiggled down, leaves crunching beneath us, so we could lie against each other—and that's when Snowball decided he'd had enough. He turned into a little yapping dynamo, barking in our ears and licking our faces. When he tried to burrow under my head, we burst out laughing, gave up and sat back against the tree. Snowball immediately leaped into Jack's lap, stretched up onto his chest and went to sleep. Lucky dog. Jack had his hand cupped over the little dog's back, and the whole scene was just...

"Hey, Jack," I said, "can I draw you?"

"What—you mean now?"

"Yeah. You and Snowball, just like that. Seems like you're stuck in that position for a while anyway. And I need to submit five sketches a week to Ms. Purcell."

He smiled. "Sure, go for it."

I ran back to the house and pulled my sketchbook and pencil out of my bag, then sat down by Jack and got to work. I was shy at first about drawing him, but once I got into it my hesitancy fell away. I just thought about the kink of Snowball's fur, and the way his head nestled under Jack's Adam's apple, and how the tips of Jack's fingers disappeared as they curled around the dog's spine…

Time went on, the light got lower, and Jack was being the most awesome model. He didn't move or complain or hardly even blink, and it was a long time before it occurred to me that he actually looked kind of weird.

I put down my sketchbook and stared at him. He didn't notice I'd stopped drawing—didn't even glance over. He just sat there motionless, his expression blank.

"Jack?"

He didn't answer, and now I was scared. I didn't know anything about his diabetes, I realized, not really. It was just part of his life—already I didn't even really notice it. I'd seen him suck down a juice box when he was "low" and knew he carried glucose tablets in his pocket all the time. Was he low now? I ran over and grabbed his shoulders.

"JACK!"

## JACK

*I don't believe it. I'm here again.*

*I'm here again, and it's just the same: the long street, the grimy, looming buildings, the mist. More mist, even.*

*And the girl.*

*I'm still not scared, not exactly, but I don't have the calm dreaminess of last time. This time there's no pretending it's just a dream. This is something really freaky, and not in a good way.*

*I walk toward the skinny girl, because what else is there to do? She sees me right away this time, and when she does her face lights up like it's Christmas Day.*

*"Jack! You came back!" she says, and for some reason her smile and warm welcome creep me out.*

*"Yeah," I say. "I'm back, but I don't know why I'm here. I don't even know how I got here."*

*"Oh." I'm up close now, so I get a good look at the strange expression that flits across her narrow face. It looks like… disappointment? Maybe even a bit hurt. Then she gives a little shrug, fastens those big blue eyes on me and smiles again.*

*"Well, no matter. You're here now, and that's lovely. I've been hoping you'd come."*

*I shuffle uncomfortably, with no idea how to respond. Then I have the really uncomfortable thought that I am worrying about my manners with a hallucination.*

*The Match Girl gazes up at me, and it strikes me that her eyes are a lot like Lucy's, and that the look in them right now is not so different from how Lucy looked at me right after we—no, no, no, I don't want to have this thought, but I'm having it anyway.*

"Jack," she says—and suddenly I don't like her using my name, wish I'd never offered it—"you're the first person to ever visit me. I never knew how lonely it was here until you came. So of course I'm happy to see you. Will you stay and talk longer this time?"

"Well." I clear my throat, stalling. For the first time, it occurs to me that I have no idea how to go home, or wake up, or whatever. And now I am scared. "The thing is, um— look, won't you tell me your name? I can't very well call you Match Girl."

Her face shuts down and hardens for a second. "Other people do."

I backpedal. Somehow it doesn't seem like a good idea to make her mad. "Okay, that's cool." Her expression changes to confusion, and I realize cool is probably not part of her vocabulary. "No problem, Match Girl. See, I don't seem to have any control over this, coming or going. I just…find myself here."

I'm actually trying not to think about this fact—that way lies panic. And in groping for a different thought, I get a great idea. I'll take a pic, and then when I get home—if I get home, my mind corrects, and I shove that word away, hard—when I get home, if the photo's there I'll know I didn't imagine her.

I reach into my jeans pocket, but there's no phone. I pat down my other pockets, come up blank and think it's *probably in my jacket or backpack. Then I realize I don't have my meter either. It's almost always in my front right pocket. I grope at my beltline—no pump. What the hell?*

*"What's wrong?" asks the Match Girl. She's watching my performance with bright interest.*

*"I'm missing some things—some important things." I do feel the familiar lump from my glucose tabs, but there's something odd about it, and when I pull them out the tablets are in a little cloth bag instead of a plastic tube.*

*The girl nods knowingly. "Pickpockets. They're thick on this street." Then, puzzled, she corrects herself. "Were thick. There's nobody now. What have you lost?"*

*I open my mouth and then realize she won't have the slightest idea what I'm talking about. Instead I ask, "What year is this, and what city?"*

*She rolls her eyes. "Copenhagen, of course. And it was 1823 when I died, but that was some time ago."*

*She says it so casually—when I died—and now my floaty little don't-worry-this-can't-really-be-happening bubble bursts, and I'm so scared I'm afraid my legs might buckle. I'm in a time warp with a dead girl and none of the technology that keeps me alive came with me, maybe because it doesn't actually exist here. I start to shake, and I'm shaking so hard my head's nodding back and forth and—*

"JACK!"

—and I'm staring up into wide blue eyes, but they're Lucy's eyes. She's standing over me, shaking my shoulders and shouting my name and looking terrified.

⁓

"I'm okay," I blurted out.

Lucy kind of collapsed with relief, rolling back into the leaves.

"Oh God. Christ, you scared me." She sat up and eyed me carefully. "You sure you're okay?"

I gave a shaky nod. I wasn't *that* sure. Something was definitely not right. I felt my waistband and was relieved to find my pump where it should be, clipped to my belt loop.

Lucy raced on. "I couldn't remember—I wasn't sure what to do. Should I go get a Coke or something?"

I shook my head. "That's not the problem. Let's go inside—I'm getting cold." I *was* cold, but that wasn't what was making me shiver so hard. I felt like a vibrating cell phone.

Inside, I was glad to see we had the house to ourselves for once. We went straight to my room anyway, like we both felt the need for a small private space, and sat on my bed. Lucy took my hand and trained her eyes on me. "So what happened out there? You were totally away with the fairies, as my grampa would say."

I'd been away *somewhere,* all right. And I just blurted it out. "I had this really weird experience. It's the second time it's happened. I'm starting to think I have a brain tumor or something."

She listened quietly until I started talking about the girl, and then her features morphed into some drama-class parody of astonished shock. When I was little, one of our babysitters was this guy Andrew, who used to bring his old *Ghostbusters* figures for us to play with. My favorite had "fright features"—*Jaw drops, eyes bug out!* Lucy looked like that. She thought I'd totally lost it, I realized, but she didn't say anything. Instead she yanked her sketchbook out of her bag and started flipping pages frantically.

Then she thrust it at me. There she was—same clothes, same frail frame, same eyes too big for her pinched little face. Lucy had drawn the Match Girl.

"I saw her." Her voice was so quiet I had to lean in to hear her. "On my way home the day I met you, I saw her."

# SEVEN

## KLARA

My Jack came to see me again. He's just as handsome as I remembered, and I'm certain now he's a gentleman, despite his odd clothes. His shoes are strange, but they look very new, and he uses words I've never even heard. But he's not one of those gentlemen who look down on the small folk like we are vermin or criminals; not Jack. He speaks to me so politely, like I was a fine lady. Only he doesn't say "Miss" or "m'Lady," of course; anyone can see I'm not really a lady.

He said he didn't know why he came, but I think that was bashfulness. He must have come to see me— why else would he come here? There's nothing here but me. To think that he was missing me the way I miss him— oh! Nobody has ever missed me, not ever!

He went away so quickly though, and then the street was emptier and lonelier than ever before. As night came on, the mist oozed out of the alleys and hung in little tendrils over the street, and I had that feeling—the idea that if it got thick enough and swirled right around my feet, it might swallow me up, and then I'd be gone too. But it's just a feeling. Since I met Jack my thoughts have been clearer. The mist is just mist. The reason the people are all gone is that they died. One by one, young or old, they died. But when they died, they left—to heaven or hell, I suppose. Perhaps the mist is filling in for all the people who have left.

Only I stayed, just as I stayed the night I died. I don't know why or how I stayed, but I know I don't want to disappear into the mist—especially now that I've met Jack. He'll come back, and he'll stay longer next time. I'm sure of it.

I had a thought after he left, a thought so exciting it makes me feel bright and strong.

I don't think Jack is dead.

# EIGHT

## LUCY

Bugs and spiders, up and down my spine.

Something beyond weird was happening. I couldn't even seem to find any words to talk about it, and I guess neither could Jack, because he just sat there, gaping at my sketch.

The silence stretched out, and then Jack looked at me kind of wild-eyed and blurted out, "How did she *get* here?"

Like I would know. But as I thought about it, I answered slowly, "You know, I'm not sure she *was* here—not the way you mean. She was sort of floating over the river, and she didn't seem to see anything around her." I paused, wondering whether to add the part about her saying his name, and decided that would just freak him out. More, I mean. "Maybe I just somehow saw her," I finished lamely.

"But who is she? Why am I going there? Why are you seeing her?" Jack's elbows were on his knees, and he dropped his head into his hands. "None of this makes any fucking sense."

Resourceful Take-Charge Lucy didn't have a clue what to do. So I said the first thing that came into my head. "Let's just go through the whole thing from the start, everything you can remember, and maybe…" I trailed off because I couldn't actually come up with anything this might accomplish.

But it seemed to make Jack feel better. "I was in math class," he began.

## JACK

I hadn't got very far into telling Lucy about my first Weird Encounter when she stopped me.

"She was selling matches?"

"Yeah. I asked her name, and she looked at me like I was a moron and said, *I'm the match girl.*"

"Oh my god, it's the Little Match Girl!"

"Is that supposed to mean something?"

"You know, 'The Little Match Girl'! The story?" She looked at me, all expectation, and got nothing but a blank. Reconsidered. "No. I guess when I think about it, it's probably not common kids' knowledge."

"So what's it about?"

"It's old—kind of a fairy tale, I guess. It gave me nightmares when I was a kid."

Of course it did. Too much to hope that it would be a *nice* story. "You better tell me about it."

Lucy hesitated, glanced at her watch and said, "It's just five. If we leave right now, we can catch the bus back to my place. I'm pretty sure I still have the book. I think we should read it."

I was on my feet before she'd finished talking. I wanted to see the book, yes, but I also wanted to get out of the house. I wasn't sure where everyone was, but I knew at least some of them would be back for dinner—and I was so not ready to talk to anyone but Lucy.

I scrawled a note, and we hustled out the door. Buses don't run too often in this town, and the routes are often pretty roundabout. Luckily, Lucy and I lived at opposite ends of the same route. We jogged the two blocks to Riverside and then stood around for ten minutes, wondering if the bus was late or if we'd missed it. "They're always late this time of day," said Lucy, and, sure enough, it came lumbering into view. We didn't talk at all for the entire ride north along the river. It's like we were just holding the interrupted conversation in our heads, waiting to pick it up again.

Lucy lived on a street full of tiny one-story brick houses, strung together in pairs or foursomes. They weren't really old, like my house, but the trees were pretty big, and the houses had grown distinguishing features like front porches and back additions.

Lucy's house had a bright-blue front door and a small concrete stoop. Inside, it was tidy but sort of bare. Of course, I was used to the debris of four people—including two slobby boys—so probably it was just normal. Lucy led me straight to her room.

It was way different there. The walls were covered in her artwork—lots of sketches and a few finished paintings that I'd have loved to spend time really looking at. Clothes and books were scattered around. A hand-lettered sign on her dresser mirror said *BE WHO YOU ARE.* I bent to take a look at the photos on the dresser while Lucy rummaged in a bookshelf. There was one of Lucy at about five, between her mom and dad, holding their hands while they swung her in the air. She looked like a little elf child with her big eyes and heart-shaped face and swirl of dark hair. They all looked happy.

"Here it is." Lucy sat on the bed with an old hardcover book and flipped pages. I squeezed in beside her. She still smelled like fresh air and leaves, and all I really wanted was to kiss her neck and hold her against me and feel her shoulder bones, like little wings, under my hands. I felt a sudden flare of anger that the memory of our first kiss would always be eclipsed by the weirdness that happened next.

"Okay, 'The Little Match Girl,' by Hans Christian Andersen." Lucy laid the book in my lap, open at an illustration of a young girl in ragged clothing, standing on a dark, snowy street. It didn't look exactly like *my* Match

Girl, but I recognized the scene, all right, and it spooked me enough that I forgot about Lucy's neck.

"Andersen...that's my mom's last name."

"Really?" Lucy shot me a quick glance. "He wrote tons of famous fairy tales. This one though—it's pretty dark."

We read through it together, and when we were done I just shook my head. "He wrote that for kids? No wonder you had nightmares."

Lucy snorted. "I guess we're supposed to be all happy she got her reward in heaven. But really, it's a story about a poor abused girl who freezes to death while rich people ignore her."

Then we went quiet, each of us, I guess, trying to put the story together with the Match Girl I'd met and find some kind of answer there. It was impossible.

And then I went low. I didn't notice at first—I was feeling too weird already to notice I was feeling weird— but I clued in when my fingers started trembling. Then that starving-but-pukey wave rolled through me. I groped in my pocket for my glucose, stuffed three sugar tablets into my mouth and pulled out my meter. I could feel the sweat standing out on my forehead now—never a good sign. I tested at 2.7, low enough to make me a bit loopy. With everything that had gone on, I realized, I hadn't tested or eaten anything since lunch. I popped another sugar tab.

"Jack? You okay?"

"Yeah, I'm just low." I tried to smile reassuringly though I felt like crap. "I'll be okay, but I should eat something more than sugar. You got anything like crackers and peanut butter?"

By the time she ran back with a sleeve of Premium Plus and a jar of PB, I was already perking up. "Sorry if I scared you. It doesn't usually take me by surprise like that." I felt like I could inhale the entire contents of a fridge, but I'd probably given Lucy enough excitement for one day. I made four cracker-and-peanut-butter sandwiches and resisted the urge to cram them all into my mouth at the same time.


## LUCY

At least Jack going low broke the spell, or we might have sat there, baffled, on the bed forever.

"Let's make dinner," I suggested. "At least, if I can find anything to make." It was Thursday. My mom usually shops on Friday, her day off, so the cupboards were pretty bare.

We found decent salad fixings, odds and ends of vegetables, a frozen ham (when did my mother think we would ever eat such a big ham?) and two frozen blocks of tofu. I looked at them glumly. "I bought three of these because I thought I should eat more vegetarian," I confessed, "but I don't really know what to do with it."

I'd choked my way through a stir-fry dotted with tasteless white blobs and given up. I looked in the cupboard where we keep the canned stuff. "There might

be some tomato sauce in here—there's always spaghetti."
I was embarrassed—here was Jack at my house for the
first time, and I couldn't even make him a decent dinner.
His kitchen was always full of food.

But he pulled the tofu out of the freezer. "This is
good," he said. "We've got onions, peppers, some other
stuff—I'm thinking tofu scramble. You got potatoes?
Maybe with hash browns and salad?" He caught my
look. "My mother was vegetarian for years—haven't
you noticed what a total ex-hippie she is? Not even ex.
We eat vegetarian a lot." He was rummaging in the
fridge, pulling out ingredients. "How about I do the
tofu, and you do the rest?"

We set to work. He asked for maple syrup and limes
(which we didn't have), garlic and soy sauce and brown
sugar (which we did). He nuked the tofu, squeezed
it till it bled a bunch of clear liquid into the sink and
sliced it up. Then he whipped up this brown concoction,
set the tofu to soak in it and started chopping onions.
I just watched him, sort of entranced. I'd never realized
how sexy a man wielding a kitchen knife could be. Jack
paused and glanced up, as if he could feel my eyes on
him, and my face flushed. You'd think I'd been caught
peeping at him in the shower. Ridiculous.

"Um, right, potatoes," I muttered and busied myself
washing and peeling. "How do you do hash browns—cut
them up really small and fry them?"

"Sure. Unless there's something else you want to do?"

So polite, not wanting to take over. I smiled and dropped a little curtsy. "Nope. I'm happy to take orders here."

I chopped up the potatoes and set them frying with a sprinkle of the onions. Then I asked Jack to walk me through the tofu, and he told me about marinating it so it takes on some flavor.

We had so much fun cooking together. Studiously ignoring what had happened before, we just concentrated on playing house. I ripped up lettuce, and Jack fried the vegetables and tofu together, then poured some of the leftover marinade over the pan.

It was so yummy—the tofu salty and sweet and a bit crispy on the outside, all mixed in with the onions and peppers.

"To the chef." I held up my water glass and we clinked.

"*Merci, Mademoiselle. Tu es charmante.*" He laid it on with a thick accent, then grinned. "Actually, I can only cook about three other things. It's lucky you didn't ask me to make the ham."

# NINE

## JACK

Thank God for Lucy. I'd have been *really* going crazy if not for her. By the time I left her house I actually felt pretty normal—normal enough, anyway, to give her a long and heartfelt kiss goodbye.

"You sure you have to go home now?" she murmured, and that's all it took to set everything racing. *Stay, stay,* my body commanded. But instead I nodded reluctantly.

"I really do need to tell my parents what's going on, and I don't want it to be too late." You told Lucy, you can tell them, my Good Boy mind insisted. They would probably march me straight to the hospital for a tox screen. But I couldn't think of a better plan.

It was a long walk home from Lucy's, and I was about halfway there when my phone rang. I peered at the screen. Dad.

"Hey, Dad, I'm almost home."

But he wasn't calling about me. "Jack, listen. We're at the police station with Noah."

"With Noah? Why, what happened?"

"I'll tell you when we see you."

"Is he all right?"

"Oh, yeah, sorry. Noah's fine. He got himself in some trouble though, so we're trying to sort it out. We might not be home for a couple of hours."

"Oh. Okay. Anything I can do?"

"No, that's okay. Don't worry—nobody's hurt. Just— your mom and I forgot to leave a note and didn't want you to worry about us." I hear Mom's voice saying something in the background. "Oh, and can you let the dog out?"

"Yeah, of course. I'll be home in, like, twenty minutes."

Geez. Noah was only thirteen, and I'd never known him to get into anything bad. On the other hand, I'd been pretty tied up in my own life, and Noah wasn't a big talker. I didn't really know much about what he'd been up to, apart from the hockey.

When I got home I let out Snowball and then went into Noah's room. I didn't search his closet or anything; I just kind of looked around, wondering what was going on and vaguely thinking I might see something that would give me a clue. Of course, I didn't—it was just

Noah's room. He'd seemed okay to me. A couple of times lately he'd had some kids at the house, and they looked, I dunno, normal enough.

My wandering took me back to my room, where the rats were clinging to the side of the cage, begging to come out and play. The cage was getting pretty stinky, and I needed something to kill time while I waited, so I let them run around on my bed while I cleaned the cage. I took my time and did a good job, wiping the pee off both levels and washing the water bottle and food dish. When I was done it was still only ten o'clock.

I felt like I shouldn't interrupt whatever was going on, and Dad had said Noah was fine, but I couldn't help feeling uneasy. I hoped Noah knew enough not to get mouthy with the police. Finally I fired off a quick text to Dad. **Everything okay?**

It took a few minutes, but soon I got the *ping* of a reply. **Yes. Home soon.**

~ ❦ ~

I couldn't read my parents' faces too well, but Noah's expression was embarrassment mixed with shame rather than oh-my-god-my-life-is-ruined, which made me feel a whole lot better. He avoided my eye, ducked his head and bolted for his room. My parents flopped down on the livingroom couch, emitting twin sighs.

"So?"

They exchanged glances: *You tell him. No, you tell him—I'm too fried. How much should we tell him?* Finally, my dad straightened up and gave this baffled little laugh. Not an amused laugh.

"Noah was with some kids who got caught stealing stuff out of parked cars."

"You're kidding me." I pictured a gang methodically stripping all the cars in a parking lot, so could not picture my little brother as part of it.

"That's what I said."

The long version of the story made more sense. Noah had been at a kid's house with some other guys after school, ostensibly working on a project. But they got fooling around and by five hadn't got too far, so they decided to keep working and then go for pizza. By the time they were walking back from the little neighborhood plaza where they'd eaten, it was dark, and I guess one kid started checking the doors on cars parked on the street as they walked by. And then he tried a few cars that were parked in driveways, and he actually got into some and cleaned the change out of the cup holders.

My dad sighed again. "He was caught when a woman flicked on her outdoor lights and stepped out with the recycling bin. The light caught him straightening up from her car with a handful of CDs. She identified him to the cops by his red hair." A tired smile. "So he was caught red-handed and red-haired."

"But Noah?"

"Sounds like none of the other kids, including Noah, had anything to do with it. But they didn't stop him either."

I thought back to some of the dumb things my friends had done over the years. "That's not always as easy as it sounds. What were they supposed to do— tackle him?" I was mad, all of a sudden—mad for my quiet, awkward brother, who had probably been relieved to have made some friends, only to find himself knee-deep in this assholery.

"Mmm." Dad didn't sound convinced. "Anyway, we'd have been home sooner if Noah hadn't refused to, as he put it, *rat anyone out*. It was the kid himself, once he realized he'd been clearly identified, who admitted he'd acted on his own. And the woman confirmed the other kids had been out on the street."

Poor Noah. Of course he didn't want to be the new kid whose claim to fame was throwing someone to the cops.

And that's why I didn't tell my parents—*again*— about my trip down the rabbit hole.


## LUCY

After Jack left I got into the shower and stood under it for a long time. At first I was having nice smitten-girl thoughts, picturing how the muscles in his forearms flexed as he chopped vegetables, and the lovely way his whole face opens up when he smiles. Remembering our kisses. Okay, and fantasizing about having him in the shower with me—of course I was. But honestly, I was kind of glad he wasn't actually in there yet. I had some not-so-great encounters with guys when I was playing teen runaway, and the fact that Jack wasn't pushing things along too fast made me feel like I'd be able to trust him when the time came. Of course, there had been a fairly major distraction to deal with…

And with that my whole mood changed. She hovered in my mind, floating with her lost eyes and skinny legs, and although I did pity her, I had the sudden conviction that the Match Girl was not just sad—she was dangerous. The shower closed in on me, claustrophobic, and I was reminded of an old movie called *Psycho*. Ali had made me watch it with her; her dad is a film nerd with a huge DVD collection. You'd never believe a black-and-white movie with a corny soundtrack and no special effects would be scary, but it's impossible to take a shower after watching that movie and not feel a bit freaked. That was how I felt now. I slammed shut the taps and yanked open the curtain, feeling stupid because of course she wasn't there. Still, I barely toweled off before jamming my legs into my pj's, feeling dumb again as the flannel stuck to the dampness, but damn, being naked is not a good thing when you're spooked.

Then I checked the lock on the door and walked around turning on lights, trying to dispel every dark corner. I wondered how things were going for Jack, if his parents were sitting in Emerg with him at this very moment, and I almost texted him but decided I shouldn't interrupt. I made a pot of tea and sat at the kitchen table, waiting for my mom to get home.

～⚬～

The look on Mom's face—surprised, then sort of cautious, like she was girding herself for bad news—didn't exactly encourage me to pour my heart out. But I really just wanted company anyway. And I could hardly blame her—I was always in my room when she got home, probably not asleep but reading or listening to music or finishing up homework. She'd poke her head in the door and say, *Goodnight. Don't stay up too late*, and that would be that. Hard to say which of us was avoiding the other.

"Hi. You're still up," she said. A+ for observation.

"I made some tea—want a cup?"

She started to shake her head, then stopped herself. "Sure."

I was surprised, and a little annoyed, at how glad I was when she said yes. It was just a stupid cup of tea, for God's sake.

We sat together, and I poured for us both. It was my third or maybe fourth cup, but I didn't care. Then my mom decided she was hungry too and made toast fingers for us both. That felt nice, a cozy remnant from my childhood.

We did How Was Your Day and Hasn't the Weather Been Nice and then my mom said carefully, "You don't often wait up for me. Not that I'm complaining, but—was there something you wanted to talk about?"

*Yes, Mom, this boy and I are having a joint hallucination of a dead girl from an old story, and we don't know what to do about it.* I didn't want to tell her that, didn't want to ruin this nice almost-normal mother-daughter moment. Instead, I smiled at her and confessed, "I met a boy at school I really like. He cooked me dinner tonight."

She grinned at me, and even though I could also see the relief on her face, it was still a nice, genuine smile, like she was really glad for me. She asked me the obligatory mom questions and teased me a bit, and then she yawned, looked at her watch and said, "I'm beat. And you should get to bed too." As she headed toward the bathroom, she called over her shoulder, "Turn the lights out before you turn in. It's lit up like Christmas in here."

I went to bed and texted Jack.

# TEN

## JACK

You know how every time there's a freak storm or a huge earthquake or a flash flood, everyone starts talking about climate change, and then the next day the sun comes out and there's something else on the news and we all forget about it again? I keep thinking that people—if there are any left—will look back on our time and wonder how we kept ignoring the obvious.

And that's what it was like for me with the Match Girl. This completely weird, inexplicable, scary thing had happened, but the next day I still had to get up and go to school and then go to rehearsal for *The Importance of Being Earnest*. Once past the silent tension at breakfast—Noah shuffling down, shooting me an imploring look that I easily translated as *Just. Don't. Say. Anything*; Mom grimly focused on lunches and dishes—it became a day like any other. Sam Heffernan, not the sharpest knife in the drawer, set fire to his own shirt with his Bunsen burner in chemistry, causing brief panic followed by high hilarity. Practicing how to kiss Amelia Patel in the play was kind of odd but in a really normal way—two awkward kids trying to act like kissing a random person onstage was no big deal. And by the end of the day, the Match Girl was already fading back into unreality.

Lucy and I, by unspoken agreement, avoided all talk of "it" at school. Honestly, I was reluctant to bring the Match Girl up at all. It's not that I believed just talking might summon her or something—not really. I just felt like maybe it was better to let it lie.

And anyway, I had better things to do with Lucy. Who wouldn't rather make out with their new girlfriend than sit around beating their brains against an insoluble problem?

There was also the Halloween party to talk about. A kid named Jordan, whom I barely knew but who seemed okay, was having a party in his parents' barn on the outskirts of town. He seemed to be inviting everyone he crossed paths with—including me, when we nearly collided on the stairwell. "Hey, man, you should come to my party!" And then he was gone, hurtling down the stairs like a SWAT team was after him. It was definitely the kind of potentially sketchy situation that made my parents imagine an entire Hell's Angels chapter showing up at the door—but intriguing. City kids don't get to party in barns too often.

"So will there be, like, hay and stalls and stuff?" I asked. The subject had come up at lunch, and Rafe and Alex, who knew Jordan better, allowed that they'd like to go.

"No, man," Alex scoffed. "It's sort of half-finished, like a bad basement rec room. And they have a couple of big electric heaters, so if we get enough people in there, it should stay fairly warm."

"What about costumes?" Rafe asked.

Alex looked blank, then slightly horrified. "Oh no. Shit. I friggin' hate costumes."

"What? Why?"

I didn't need to ask to know Rafe *loved* costumes. He'd taken every drama course he could and was trying to get into the Ryerson performing arts program—costumes were a second skin for him.

"I never know what to wear. Always end up looking like a tool, and uncomfortable as hell all night. Itching or sweating to death or all"—Alex made a struggling gesture that reminded me of Noah when he was little, fighting his car-seat straps—"bound up." He looked morose. "Annie will harass me into wearing one, won't she?" Annie was his girlfriend, and she did seem like she might put a lot of stock in costumes.

"Don't worry, man. We'll help you find something." Rafe looked at me confidently. "Won't we?"

"Yeah, sure." *Ha*. I had no idea what to wear myself. "Let's just make sure that costumes are actually happening though, right?"

## LUCY

I was lukewarm on the party from the get-go. I'm not a fan of big, crowded events full of drunk people, and out in the country it's not always so easy to get home when you've had enough. But it would be more fun with Jack there, I thought—he wouldn't be getting totally wasted, and his easiness with people would help me relax. So I was actually disappointed when the achy headache I went to bed with the night before the party bloomed into a fever high enough to keep me shivering and sweating in bed, counting down the hours until I could take the next dose of Tylenol.

My mom was already at work when I woke up the next morning; she'd left me a note reminding me that she was doing a shift for somebody named Wanda who had a wedding to attend. I tottered to the bathroom, wishing I had my granny Kay's walker to hold me up, and grabbed my phone on the way back to bed. I called the café to tell them I couldn't make my shift. Then I huddled under the covers and sent Jack a miserable text:

**SICK!!! Cant go 2nite. Just leave me here to die. XO**

It was too bad, I thought, as I clamped my eyes shut and willed myself to sleep. I wouldn't even need makeup for my costume—I pretty much already looked like Zombie Girl.

## JACK

Alex's dad pulled into the turnaround at the end of the long laneway, and we piled out of the car into a frosty

cold night. He leaned out the driver's-side window.
"Okay, guys, behave yourselves, eh? Just 'cause you're
partying in a barn doesn't mean you should act like you
were raised in one." He snorted at his own joke.

"Dad." Alex looked pained. "Thanks for the ride.
We'll be cool."

Mr. Curcio had already ensured we had the numbers
of both cab companies and enough cash between us to
share a fare back into town. My mother would approve.
We'd had a testy exchange about this party, which she
was clearly envisioning as Country Kids Gone Wild, and
about my own personal-safety precautions.

*"You should give one of your friends the glucagon, and
teach them to use it."*

Glucagon is a rescue treatment for a low so bad I'm
unconscious. I pictured a drunk friend trying to plunge
that fat glucagon needle through my jeans into my thigh.
No thanks.

*"Mom, it's only ten minutes out of town. They can just
call an ambulance."*

*"What if the ambulance is delayed?"*

*"You never worried about that in Montreal. They can be
delayed anywhere. And anyway, I'm not going to need it."*

Big sigh. But she'd given up, and here I was.

We went up to the house with another clump of kids
who had just arrived and went through an odd little secu-
rity check with Jordan's parents, who made us all introduce
ourselves (I guess to make sure we weren't party crashers)

and asked a girl who had driven to deposit her keys in a bowl. Presumably, there would be some kind of sobriety test before she got them back. Then we were ushered out the back door and pointed toward a looming dark shape. The moon, white and full in a sky darker than you ever see in the city, lit up the path better than the handful of feeble little solar lights stuck in the grass along the way.

When we dragged open the barn door, a wave of noise washed over us. The music was poppy crap (IMHO, ha-ha) but loud and danceable. I glanced into the cavernous space, wondering how they'd managed to fill the place with sound, and saw a bank of speakers arrayed along what I guessed would have been the floor of the original hayloft. Impressive. A couple dozen kids were there already, standing around in clumps, yelling at each other over the music, swaying but not dancing yet—and there was room for plenty more.

We made our way farther into the room, the old carpets underfoot changing color and texture as we progressed. We found Jordan, who waved at us and pointed toward the back wall, where we found a pile of coats and a big old fridge.

"Sweet!" Rafe yelled. "Cold beer tonight." We unloaded our cans of Pabst from our backpacks, and Rafe tucked them into the fridge. *Thank you, Alex's older brother.*

"Jack?" Rafe held out a can, his grin turned into a hideous leer by his Joker makeup. His costume put my zombie (shredded old paint clothes and face paint from the kit we'd used when we were kids) to shame, but on the other hand, I looked damn good beside Alex, who had thrown on a plaid shirt and tuque to become a half-assed lumberjack. Annie, hanging on his arm, had on this floor-length black velvet dress that she said had belonged to her grandmother. Even I, fashion-challenged as I was, could tell it was spectacular, and she was wearing just enough vampire makeup to make her look exotic and awesome.

I didn't intend to drink much—despite what I'd told my mom, we were more like twenty minutes out of town, and I had no interest in testing the local ambulance service. But there were a lot of kids here I didn't know, and a little social lubricant wouldn't hurt.

"Thanks, man." I cracked the tab and took a long swallow. Too bad Lucy couldn't come. I really wanted to dance with her tonight.

~ ⁂ ~

I was most of the way through my beer, and the "dance floor" under the speaker bank was filling up, when a blond, willowy girl in a skimpy black-and-white outfit planted herself before me.

"Hi, Jack."

"Hi. Um…Becky, right?"

"Geez, I'd have hoped you wouldn't have to guess." She did a fake pout, tipping her head to look up at me from under the drama of her eyelids. I saw the little white frilly cap pinned to the back of her head, and the light went on.

"Ah—the French maid!"

"*Mais oui, Monsieur.*" She stepped close and put her mouth to my ear so I could hear over the music. "Come and dance with me." She clamped her hand firmly around mine and led me over to the dancers.

Becky was a good dancer but not comfortable to dance with—you know how that is? She stared at me too much, got too close, demanded too much, if that makes sense. Always wanting some reaction. So it was a relief when after a couple of tunes she fanned her cleavage and yelled, "It's too hot. Let's go for a drink."

It was quieter at the fridge. "Oh, I just loved that last song," Becky said. "So great for dancing. Who was it, do you know?" She had a beautiful smile—perfect teeth and a little dimple that puckered up in one corner.

"That was Lady Gaga, wasn't it?"

She wrinkled up her nose. "Ew. That meat-dress thing. Why do people have to be so *weird*?"

I shrugged and opened the fridge. It really irritates me when people say things like that. Not that I was a fan of wearing meat or even much liked Gaga's music. "Beer or...?"

"Beer, of course." I took one for myself too, in self-defense.

"Speaking of weird, Jack." Becky swigged her beer and smiled sweetly at me. "I've been seeing you with Lucy

Sullivan a lot lately." She waited, eyebrows raised, as if she expected me to deny it.

I just nodded, knowing already I wasn't going to like where this was going—and that I didn't like Becky what's-her-name.

"Well, it's nice of you to befriend her and everything, but Jack, you're new, so you wouldn't know she has a *history*. You don't want to get too wrapped up with a girl like that."

"A girl like *what*, Becky?" I was mad now, mad enough that I couldn't quite keep the hostility out of my voice.

She took a little step back. "Hey, I'm just trying to help you get off on the right foot. Lucy's messed up. And there are lots of nice girls here who'd like to get to know you." She stepped in quickly and planted one on my mouth before I could recoil.

"Think about it, Jack."

I watched her melt back into the crowd in her perfect rented costume, and then I tossed down half my beer to try to get rid of the bad taste she'd left behind.

# ELEVEN

## KLARA

Really, I think I must have been asleep before I met Jack—asleep for years and years. But I'm awake now. Some days I wish I wasn't, because I didn't realize before how lonely and tiresome it is to just stand here day in and day out. But to be able to think and wish and plan again—that part is wonderful.

I realized just a little while ago that nobody was ever, ever going to buy any matches. How would they? There is nobody here to buy them. So there is no need for me to go on selling them, is there? And nobody to punish me if I use them myself.

But it was only today that I had my best idea so far. I was looking at my matches, thinking that the match head looked a bit like a tiny person's head. And then I remembered something.

Old Mad Gerda. That's what they called her, though not to her face. She was a fearsome sight, with her broomstraw gray hair stuck out every which way and her wandering eye and the one leg shriveled and weak. She worked for a time just over there, beside that lamppost, selling love charms and fertility potions. I heard men muttering that she'd sell worse too, if asked, and once when a constable ran her off the square he called her an "old witch" and said in his papa's day she'd have been burned at the stake. But even he, I noticed, didn't whack her with his stick, not even once. People believed in her charms.

For her most expensive love charms, she made little dolls. Little scrappy things they were—just sticks lashed together and bits of cloth. I saw a customer laugh scornfully when she brought one out. But she laid her old claw hand on his arm, and I heard her explain how he should bring her something of the lady's, some hair or even a scrap of clothing, and she would bind it to the doll, and then when he possessed the doll, he would have power over the lady.

So that's what I'm going to do. I'll make a little matchstick Jack doll of my very own. Jack will come back one day, I know he will. And when he does, all I need to do is get something of his to keep. Before I wouldn't have known how, but now that I'm awake, I'm sure I can find a way. And then...well, I'm not sure how to do a binding, exactly. But I mean to try.

# TWELVE

## LUCY

I got up for a bit around dinnertime. I felt floaty, but not in a good way. Like my head wasn't quite attached to my body. My mom had come home armed with soup and Popsicles, and she fixed me a "sick meal" that tasted pretty good. After that I huddled on the couch for a while to get a change of scene, but the TV made my head hurt, and by eight o'clock I was back in bed. I just lay there feeling shivery and sick, but gradually the Tylenol kicked in and I fell asleep.

Crazy dreams. I was chasing that junkie guy through the city, slashing at him with a broken bottle the size of a baseball bat...falling through the sky into a field of solar panels, wondering calmly if I'd get electrocuted if I broke through one...trying to ride on a bus, but my different body parts kept growing and shrinking—like Alice, only all disconnected.

And then, oh God, there she was. I was surrounded by gray, swaddled in it, floating in it, and it was the most peaceful and comfortable I'd felt since getting sick—until I saw that she was there too.

She wasn't standing with her matches, the way Jack and I had both seen her before. She was crouched down, hunkered over something, her thin hair falling forward into her face. I thought, I don't want to see what she's doing there, but the words had no sooner crossed my mind than I was floating in closer, like someone had pressed the Zoom button.

She was fiddling with some matchsticks, her mouth working in concentration as she laid them in a pattern. I was surprised at how big they were—maybe four inches or so. Not like any match I'd ever used. She yanked at the edge of her shawl and pulled out an end of yarn, biting it off with her teeth. Then she set to tying the sticks together.

I peered closer, and suddenly the spiders were back in full force. My stomach knotted so tight I thought I might throw up, dream or no dream. It was a stick man she was making, a little matchstick man. And though the words she was murmuring as she worked didn't surprise me at all, they still filled me with sick dismay.

"Jack, Jack, Jack. Here's my little Jack. You'll be with me always, and once I make the binding, so will my big Jack. He'll come again, yes he will. He'll come to us, little Jack."

I lurched awake in a panic, thinking, I have to warn him. When I sat up, groping for my phone, I realized I was soaked—I mean, really soaked. My T-shirt was plastered against me, the roots of my hair wet. Just gross. Once I got out in the air, it was really cold too. With a groan I stripped off my shirt and rummaged in a drawer for a new top.

Of course, he didn't answer when I called. His phone was probably in a backpack or coat pocket in a heap of other kids' packs and coats. Even if it was in his jeans, he probably wouldn't hear it over the party noise. By the time I started texting him instead, I realized the warning was kind of pointless. What was he going to do, watch out for voodoo dolls? Still, I couldn't stop. My hands were shaking as I keyed in **Just had wrst dream. I think MG is up to sth bad. Call me?**

I sat back against my pillow and realized it was wet from my sweat. So were the sheets. Ugh. Shivering, disgusted and still disturbed by what I'd seen, I thumped to the linen cupboard, looking for dry sheets.

"Everything okay?" My mom was standing in her bedroom doorway, looking bleary.

I nodded mechanically, about to fall back on my default I-don't-need-you attitude. Then I caught myself. I didn't need to be like that anymore. "I woke up all sweaty and freaked out from a dream."

She came over and felt my forehead. "Your fever's broken. It's actually a good thing."

I grunted. "I'd hate to see bad."

Mom pulled a blanket out of the cupboard and draped it around my shoulders. "Go cuddle up in this. I'll change your bed."

There was something soothing about watching her strip and remake the bed. By the time she was done, the dream was fading, and I did feel better. I was almost due for more Tylenol, so I took one and slid under the covers. I thought I should try to think about that dream, but my body had other ideas. The light was barely out when I was drifting away in the reassuring smell of clean laundry.

## JACK

So the dope was a mistake. That's obvious *now*, but at the time I wasn't thinking about the relationships between various altered states. I just wanted to enjoy myself with my new friends and avoid overdoing the beer. I was sipping a Coke, sweaty from dancing, when Alex and Annie drifted by to ask if I wanted to go get some air. The moon was high by then; I remember looking up just as the clouds covering its face shredded and blew past, and silvery light spilled down and flooded over the fields. I'd seen moonbeams on lakes lots of times but somehow never realized the same thing happens on land.

The joint Alex produced didn't seem that strong, and we didn't even finish it because the same wind whipping the clouds past the moon was whipping us down below, and Annie was freezing in her evening gown and little wrap.

But it was enough to make me a little spacey, and when we went back inside I decided I didn't feel like more dancing. Instead I laid claim to one of the few articles of furniture in the place—a big overstuffed chair with a sprung-out seat that nearly swallowed me up when I sank into it. I hunkered down and watched the party. A couple of guys were wreaking minor havoc on the dance floor, having progressed from headbanging to uninhibited flailing. Becky what's-her-name seemed to be arguing with that really tall guy from my chemistry class. She didn't look like she needed any help either— he was practically cowering. I wondered how Lucy was doing, considered digging through the pile of stuff to find my phone and decided she would be sleeping, and I shouldn't wake her. I suddenly really missed her.

The music changed to some kind of electronica, hypnotic and repetitive. The hard-core boys squinted at the speakers, shook their heads in disgust and left the floor. I let my eyes drift up, away from the press of bodies to the gray rafters high above. Looking up, you could imagine this place as a working barn, the thump of the bass and rise and fall of crowd noise replaced by the crunch of straw underfoot, the stamping hooves and munching jaws of heavy beasts. The smell of old carpet and young bodies replaced by the sharper smell of manure. It seemed nice, peaceful. I wished I could step into that earlier time, escape for a few minutes from all these people trying so hard to have fun…

⸺ ꝏ ⸺

*Oh no. Fuck. This is not where I wanted to escape to.*

*The Match Girl catches sight of me, and her expression goes through such a rapid succession of changes she looks like a face in a flip-book: blankness, then delight that crumples into something I can't read. By the time I'm close enough to talk to her, it has settled into a pretty good likeness of horror. Huh. And here I thought she'd be glad to see me.*

*"Jack! Oh, dear Jack, what's happened to you?" She stares at me in dismay, and then her expression shifts again, her eyes thoughtful. She leans in closer and says softly, "Is it plague? You needn't worry—it won't be bad for long. I'll look after you."*

*"What?" She's scaring the crap out of me—even more than usual, I mean—until I figure it out. My hand flies to my face—my green, zombified face. "No, no, I'm fine. This is just makeup." No response. "Um, face paint?"*

*She eyes me dubiously. "Face paint. To make yourself look ill?"*

*"For a party." Still the stare. "A Halloween party. Do you know Halloween?"*

*She considers. "All Hallow's Eve?"*

*"I guess. We dress up in scary costumes on Halloween."*

*More staring. She's deciding whether I'm lying or off my nut.*

*"Then you're well, truly?" Those big blue eyes search mine.*

*"Perfectly well—I promise."*

*She holds my gaze a bit longer—uncomfortably longer—and I want to look away but can't seem to, and then her face crumples. I'm shocked to see that she's actually crying. The thought floats into my head, and it's a thought I don't much like, that the Match Girl was a lot less emotional when I first met her than she is now. Then, she was kind of blank and vague. Now she seems…more alive? But how can that be?*

*She has ramped up to outright sobbing now, words coming out brokenly between gasps of breath. "I thought… oh, I thought…I was so affrighted for you, Jack…I thought you were dying!"*

*I stand there shifting my weight from one foot to the other, wondering what I should do. Once again, social awkwardness collides with surreal fear in the weirdest way. I'm not about to put my arm around her, or even touch her—but she's crying for me, and she looks smaller and lonelier than ever. Then she peeps out from between her fingers, her breath still ragged as she gradually quiets down.*

*"I'm sorry, Jack. I shouldn't be so…" She sniffs vigorously and gives a little embarrassed laugh. "I'm a terrible mess now. Would you have a handkerchief I could use?"*

*A handkerchief. "Uh…" I rummage in my pockets, checking for Kleenex. Like before, my meter and phone are gone, but I do find a promising lump at the bottom of a back pocket. I pull it out gingerly, remembering how my sugar tabs' plastic case had turned into a cloth bag—but it's just a tissue, dabbed with dark red in the corner. Paper was invented before plastic, remembers the part of my mind that is groping for something, anything, logical. "Sorry. It's a bit used. I pulled a hangnail in class and—"*

*She snatches at it eagerly. I'm kind of taken aback—it's as if she was starving and I held out a sandwich. "That's all right, Jack. I don't mind if it's a bit dirty." She sounds like it's more than all right—she sounds pleased as punch. She's mopping at her cheeks and blowing her nose loudly, and I suddenly wonder how real her "affright" actually was.*

*"There, that's better." She beams at me. "Thank you, Jack. I shall treasure this always." And she stuffs the "hand-kerchief" tenderly into her coat, patting it to make sure it's safely stowed away.*

*I have a strong feeling that I should get it back, not leave it with this strange, ghostly girl who is becoming less ghostly every time I see her. But who asks for a snotty Kleenex to be returned? So instead I say, "Well, I should be getting back now. My friends will be worried about me." She looks at me with this teasing little pout, and I realize I've already told her that I don't actually know how to get back. But I need—really, really need—to put some distance between myself and this…whatever she is, so I say goodbye and turn and march down the street, back toward the place where I usually pop into this world, as if I'm walking home. The only plan I have is to lurk there in the mist, as far away from her as I can get, until someone gets worried enough to holler me back.*

~୬୯~

But it actually worked—apparently, I *could* just walk home. Relief washed over me as I opened my eyes and found myself sunk into the big chair, with music and chatter and bodies swirling around me. A girl's over-excited shriek, followed by a cascade of laughter, rose above the general noise, and then Rafe was in front of me, his Joker grin a little smeared but still sinister.

"Hey, man, there you are! I wondered if you'd headed home or something."

"No, just taking a break. A bit stoned, I guess." *Disoriented* would have been the better word, but *stoned* worked for Rafe. He nodded knowingly.

"Ha! You'll be hungry next, so you'll like this plan. We're kind of done here—thought we might catch a cab into town now and go for pizza before heading home."

Perfect. I'd definitely had enough party, and a nice, normal pizza pit was exactly what I needed. "Yeah, I'm in." I struggled out of the chair, and we went over to rummage through the mound of clothes for our stuff. Remembering the low I had after my last trip to the Wild Side, I tested while we waited for the cab. Actually, a little on the high side this time. You just never know.

I keyed in a couple of units, giving the insulin a head start before I assaulted my body with carbs and grease, and sat back in the warm cab. The easy banter of my friends was the perfect antidote to the weirdness with the Match Girl, and I was soon laughing and feeling fine.

Annie's phone rang, and that reminded me I'd promised to check in with my mom. I dug out my phone and saw I had a message waiting. I knew what it would say without reading it—*Going to bed now. Everything okay? Mom.*

But it wasn't from Mom. It was from Lucy.

# THIRTEEN

## KLARA

My friends, he said. I never thought of Jack having friends. I thought he was alone, like me.

I don't like him having friends. They pull him away from me. "*They'll be worried,*" he said. What would they have to be worried about? He's perfectly well here with me.

No matter. Soon I won't need to bother about his friends, because we'll be together forever.

His handkerchief has blood on it! Jack's blood. That's a powerful binder, I think. I'm sure I heard Mad Gerda say that anything from the person's body—hair or nail parings but especially blood—was the best thing to use. I'm sure it will work now.

I'll bring Jack back—and this time he'll stay.

# FOURTEEN

## JACK

That night I lay in bed staring at the ceiling for what felt like hours. I was actually kind of afraid to turn out the light, if you want to know the truth. It was edging toward dawn when I finally fell asleep and past noon when I woke up. I called Lucy right away and arranged to head over to her place as soon as I'd showered and eaten.

A middle-aged woman with Lucy's small frame answered the door. Funny—Lucy had spent so much time around my family that I'd kind of started thinking she lived alone.

"You must be Jack," Lucy's mom said, offering her hand and introducing herself as Alice. I was relieved I didn't come as a complete shock.

Lucy was on the living-room couch with a blanket tucked around her. She pulled up her feet to make room for me, and I settled at the far end, pulling her feet onto my lap. "Man, you look rough."

"I'm actually a lot better. *Yesterday* I looked rough." She waved an impatient hand, sweeping that subject off the table. "I have to tell you what I saw in that dream." The sound of the vacuum down the hall told us we had privacy, at least for now.

—∽⌒—

"She's making, like, a voodoo doll? Of me?" I was remembering the night before, the Match Girl's odd behavior, and the phrase *a sinking feeling* now demonstrated its meaning in my body.

"It could have been just my fevered, delirious mind spinning out," Lucy said. "But I gotta tell you, Jack, it really felt real."

"What's this binding she was talking about?" I thought I knew, but I didn't want to be right.

"I think she meant something that would tie the doll to you."

Not good. *So* not good.

"What?" said Lucy. "Jack, what is it?"

"I gave her a Kleenex, Lucy, and it had my blood on it."

## LUCY

For the first time, Jack seemed really freaked. Honestly, I was too. At that moment I actually believed the Match Girl was real and that she was somehow plotting to kidnap Jack. And Jack just sat there looking gobsmacked.

He finally looked at me, his eyes, well, haunted. Though as soon as the word came to me I wanted to stuff it back.

"What am I going to do?"

It killed me to see him like that. Since I'd known him, he'd always been so confident and easygoing, so *sensible*. But how can sensible fight voodoo?

So Take-Charge Lucy came up with a plan, because we had to do *something*.

"We have to do some research."

"*What*? Lucy, this isn't a joke." Jack glared at me, panic just waiting to jump out.

"No, Jack, listen. We need to figure out what's going on. There has to be some kind of info about ghosts or about the magic she's trying to use. I'll get on Google, see what I can learn. What about the conditions when you went over there? Is there a pattern, or anything they all have in common? Maybe we can figure out what makes it happen. And the Match Girl herself—who is she, and why is she there? Maybe, I dunno, we can find out why Hans Christian Andersen wrote about her. And what's the connection with you?" And me, I wondered. Why had I seen her when no one else but Jack had?

Jack offered me a quick, apologetic half smile. "Okay,
sorry—it's not a dumb idea. But God, it's overwhelming.
I don't know where to start with any of it."

"I have to start with a nap." It was true—I was fading
fast, my body demanding rest. "I'm sorry, Jack. I'm still
pretty sick, I guess. But if you like, when I wake up I'll
start looking for some way of protecting you from the
kind of spell she's planning. You start looking for a pattern
in your visits to the Twilight Zone—all those science and
math courses should be good training for that."

"Okay, I can do that," he said. "And Lucy—thanks.
I mean it." He unfolded himself from the couch, leaned
down and kissed me very gently on the forehead, like a
parent kissing a sleeping baby. It was so sweet that, sick
as I was, I felt a shivery little *zing* in response. "You rest
up now," he said. "Get yourself better before heading out
on your witch hunt."

As he shrugged into his backpack and headed for the
door, I added one more assignment. "Jack? Why don't you
start researching Andersen too? I doubt you'll find much
of interest on Wikipedia, but maybe check Amazon and
see if there are any biographies of him or, even better, an
autobiography. Or see what's in the library."

He looked daunted, but nodded. "I'll give it a shot."

## JACK

Once I started looking for it, the pattern became obvious. I wanted to call Lucy right away, but it had been barely an hour since I'd left her, so I forced myself to wait another hour. More to pass the time than with any real interest, I looked up *Hans Christian Andersen* on Amazon and, sure enough, found an autobiography, a collection from his diaries and a book of letters, not to mention a bunch of biographies. None of them looked like a quick read. I bookmarked the page, hoping I wouldn't have to spend my life savings on this wild goose chase. Then I called Lucy.

"It's been happening about once a month—just under, really."

"Just under. Define just under."

"Well…" I looked at the calendar. "Around every four weeks, give or take a day or two. The first time was the second day of school—September 5. Then that time with you in the backyard—that was what, October 2 or 3? And then the Halloween party—right on the thirty-first."

"Four weeks, twenty-eight days," Lucy said and fell silent.

I waited a bit, then asked, "You there?"

"Yeah." She gave an embarrassed laugh. "I was, well, just trying to figure out if it somehow coincided with my period. You know, that's what twenty-eight days means to girls."

I nodded as if I knew. "Right."

"But of course that's dumb," she continued. "What else is—"

"The moon," I cut in. "The moon has a twenty-eight-day cycle." I had a sudden, vivid memory of the moon flooding light over the fields at the party. "It always happens on a full moon."

We digested this factoid for a bit, neither of us having a clue why it was significant but knowing without a doubt that it was.

"Well," said Lucy finally. "That means if you're lucky, and the Match Girl doesn't find some way to yank you over prematurely, we have almost a month to figure out how to keep you here."

"The month sounds hopeful. The yanking-over part, not so much." Jesus. I really didn't need to be thinking about that.

"Sorry. We shouldn't get too cocky, is all I'm saying."

"Right." As if.

"So—Hans Christian next?"

"Oh, yeah." I reported on what I'd found.

"Great," said Lucy. "That's great." She sounded as if she really thought it was great that there were more than twenty books about an old, dead fairy-tale writer. "The school library won't have anything good. The town library can surprise you though, and you can check books out. I'd start there."

"Um…I guess I'd need to get a card first."

"You don't have a library card?" She sounded truly shocked.

"Give me a break, Luce, I only just moved here."

Silence. Then, "Did you just call me *Luce*?"

"No-o-o." It was a relief to have something to laugh about.

"Stupid place is closed Sundays," she said, "but you can go online and see what they've got. If I've rejoined the living, we can go after school tomorrow."

～♌～

I got home the next day just before dinner, lugging about fifteen pounds of books.

"What've you got in there that's so heavy?" Mom asked as my backpack thudded onto the floor.

"I'm doing a research project on Hans Christian Andersen for my drama class." An easy lie. Andersen— my mom's last name. Well, no stone unturned. "You know about him, I guess?"

My mom laughed. "It's illegal to grow up in Denmark and not know about him," she said. "And I got more than my share, because my grandfather always insisted he was our ancestor. I suppose I should have read you more of his stories, but to be honest, some of them gave me the heeby-jeebies when I was little. I like Robert Munsch better."

She turned to the stove, stirring the cheese sauce. "You could set the table for me."

But I was still back at my grandfather. "Seriously? We're related?" That could be the connection—a kind of connection anyway.

My mom shrugged. "Oh, so he claimed. But every other person in Denmark is named Andersen, so we never really believed him."

I counted out the cutlery and laid it out. That stack of books seemed like it might be worth looking at after all.

## LUCY

I was good at telling Jack what to do but didn't get far with my own assignment. I tried, but I'd barely typed my first search words into Google before my head was pounding and it felt like the computer screen was beaming little shafts of pain into my eyes. I needed to crawl into bed and get better before I could be of much use to Jack. *Live to fight another day,* I told myself, and then wondered where that expression even came from. It was part of something longer that I couldn't quite pull out of the memory bank.

I lay back on the couch and closed my eyes, my mind bumbling along in the loopy, fragmented way it works when I'm sick. *Live to fight another day, or not to fight and bear the shame…*no, that wasn't right. Suddenly I heard my dad's voice, as clear as if he was in the room with me:

"*Better to fart and bear the shame than not to fart and bear the pain.*" Grinning at me like a kid as I giggled, my mom shushing him but smiling herself.

*"Daniel, don't be teaching her that..."*

Oh God. I was so little then—four, five? I'd forgotten. There was so much about my dad I'd forgotten already, and I realized with a wave of pain that had nothing to do with my headache that I'd been *trying* to forget. Kate had talked to me about grieving, and I'd cried plenty in her office, but then I'd just...put him away. Not wanting to deal with the sadness that even the happiest memory could trigger. I'm sorry, Daddy, I thought, and then I was crying.

The kitchen radio snapped off, and I heard my mom heading toward the living room. I sat up and swiped at my eyes.

"Okay, Lucy?"

"Yeah," I mumbled. "But I've got a really bad headache. Gonna head to bed."

My mom hadn't put up a single photo of my dad when we moved here. So I wasn't the only one pushing away the memories. And I really did need to sleep. I was weak and achy by the time I crawled into bed, and even with everything I had to think about, I sank into sleep as if someone had flipped a switch and turned me off.

⁓

On Monday my fever flared up again, putting me out of commission. I didn't make it to school the next day either, but Jack called that evening to report in.

"He was a weird dude, this Hans Christian Andersen. Honestly, I'm sick of him already."

"What do you mean?"

"Well, he seems cool at first, you know? Gutsy. He was born into a poor country family, but takes off at fourteen to Copenhagen, determined to be an actor. And he somehow talks his way into the choir at some big theater, and then this guy sponsors him to get an education."

"So why don't you like him?"

"Well, that's where his diaries seem to start—when he's about our age, and in school, and it's just all this angsting out about his exams and begging God to help him and worrying that he won't do well. And then I flipped through some of the later stuff, and it's like all he talks about is what important people he met and whether they were nice to him or not and who invited him to visit. It's friggin' tiresome. Oh, but Lucy, get this." Jack suddenly sounded animated. "I might be related to the guy."

"You're kidding me." Now *that* sounded more promising.

"Apparently, my great-grandfather insisted it was true, but my mom doesn't seem to think it that likely."

"Well, it's a connection anyway. Our first lead!"

"I guess..." He didn't sound convinced. "But what does it actually mean?"

"Maybe it somehow explains why she's latched on to *you*. At any rate, we're closer than we were. Time for me to start cramming Witchcraft 101." Four sick days had put me way behind on my big history assignment, but I was pretty sure I could beg an extension. Jack's problem was more urgent.

"I'll let you know what I find out tomorrow," I said.

"Think you'll be at school?"

"Almost definitely."

"Good," Jack said. "I miss you. And…" He hesitated.

"What?"

"I'm just sorry, Lucy." He sounded kind of miserable, and I really wished I was sitting right beside him then. "I feel like this thing keeps…I dunno, shoving into the place that should be just you and me being together and getting to know each other—you know? I mean, I wish we could just be having fun together."

"It's okay, Jack," I said softly. "This is getting to know each other too."

After we hung up, I googled one wacky thing after another, from *binding spells* to *exorcising ghosts*.

# FIFTEEN

## KLARA

I haven't been able to bring Jack back to me yet. At first I tried simply laying my little Jack doll on his handkerchief, but I soon realized it wasn't so simple. Mad Gerda was always muttering over her charms, saying spells, and I don't know the proper words. I was so angry then, to think all my work was for nothing—angry like I never was in life, rage rising up in me like a fire. It was a bad feeling, I suppose, yet I clung to it—I felt so alive, so powerful!

Yet when it subsided, Jack was still not here, and my little doll was. And I found I was glad I hadn't broken it in my anger. I like my little Jack—he's not Jack, not really, but he's still better than nobody.

I've been carrying him around under my coat, wrapped in the handkerchief, for some time now, though I couldn't say how long. Time is strange here—another thing I never gave a moment's thought to until Jack woke me up. But now I have brought him out again, for it's come to me that if I don't know the proper spell, I can make one up. Somebody must have made up Gerda's, so why not me? If it doesn't work, I can try another, and another...

First I am going to strengthen my Jack doll. I've torn a hole in the handkerchief—it's easily ripped—and now I am going to put it over Jack's head like the shift he wears. I am going to put the blood spot right over his heart and tie it in place. I will daub some soot at the top for his dark hair. And then I will say a spell, my own spell.

I never had anything of my own, never dared want more than a morsel of food and a safe bed. But now I do, and nobody can punish me for it. I want Jack.

I may not be able to bring him here with my doll, but sooner or later he'll come back on his own, and when he does, I'm going to keep him.

# SIXTEEN

## LUCY

I had a shift at the café after school, so Jack and I really only got to talk at lunch.

"It's crazy—you can find spells for all kinds of things." I felt like my research of the night before had only muddied the waters. "But breaking spells seems to be more complicated, and figuring out which would be the right one…" Jack's eyes were glued on me, but that didn't stop him from dispatching his sandwich with alarming speed. "I dunno, it's like, how do you find a *reputable* witchcraft source? Can anyone just follow the recipe, or do you need training? And if any of this actually works, will it work on the ghost of an imaginary character in another world?"

He nodded. "It does all seem pretty surreal. But if we're agreed that I need to take her seriously, I guess we have to blunder on."

"Right. Okay then, my impression is that doing spells is easier than breaking spells, so the first thought I had was that we could bind you to me, and it would be pretty easy to come up with something stronger than what she's got, plus your willingness would add strength, and that would keep you here while we figured out how to undo both."

To my horror, I found that I was blushing, like I was suggesting we get married or something. "But that's not ideal," I hurried on. "You shouldn't be bound to *anyone*. I'm sure we can find a spell to break the binding." I didn't tell him that any spells I had already found required something of the spellcaster's—ideally, from the spellcaster's *body*—in order to break the link to the sender.

Jack looked thoughtful rather than appalled, which was a relief. "I would definitely rather be bound to you than her." The sweet little smile he sent my way erased my embarrassment. "But I don't like the idea of setting up a tug-of-war between you and her. It seems like even if it took me out of danger, it might put *you* in her sights."

I was about to say, *I don't see how she could hurt me*, but thought twice and didn't. Clearly, the laws of what was possible did not apply here.

The phone rang the next morning just as I was getting into the shower. I stuck my head out the door until I was sure my mother had picked up and it wasn't for me. I was mostly dressed when she tapped on my door and came in.

"What's up?" I noticed her bathrobe and her bed-head hair before I took in the look on her face. "Mom, what's wrong?"

She eased herself down on my bed. "That was the hospital in Ottawa. They said...Lucy, I'm afraid your grandfather Shamus has died."

My eyes were burning with tears before her words had fully sunk in, like my body understood faster than my mind. "Oh God—how?" But I was hardly listening to the words *pneumonia, complications, underlying lung disease.* I was flashing back to when my dad died, and how one of the many things I'd been angry about was that my mother had stopped visiting his father, my Grampa Shamus. I loved my grampa and had yelled at Mom about how he was lonely and sad too. *"Lucy, I just can't,"* she'd said and left the room. I'd wanted to see my grampa because I thought it would be a bit like seeing my dad. Now I realized my mother hadn't felt able to for the same reason.

She'd started visiting again in the past year, though, and we'd made the three-hour drive to Ottawa every few months. But I looked at her now and saw guilt as well as sorrow.

"He didn't even tell me he was sick," she murmured. Then she straightened her back, sighed and looked at me straight on. "Lucy, I have to go down there and organize things. There's no one else."

"Uncle Steve?"

"They're trying to get a message to Stephen. He's overseas again—in Syria, I think." My dad's brother was a Doctors Without Borders staffer with an apparent compulsion to serve in the most dangerous and difficult conditions possible. My father had spoken of him with equal parts pride and exasperation, and I'd overheard him remark once that Steve's brief marriage had died of absenteeism.

"I guess, now that I think of it, he's not likely to be much help."

Mom shook her head. "We'll be lucky if he makes it to the funeral."

"I'll go with you." The words tumbled out of my mouth without forethought, but they felt right. She needed me.

"Oh, Lucy." Now my mom was teary, but she sniffed it back. "Thank you. It means the world to me that you offered. But you don't have to." She ran a hand through her hair in a vain attempt to smooth it down and turned to face me, her eyes direct and serious. "I know you carried too much when your dad died. You took on things no kid should have to, and I'm sorry for that." I didn't see the point of denying it, not now, so I just nodded. "But you don't have to do it again. When Daniel died, I lost the love of my life. I'm truly sad about your grampa, and a little overwhelmed at what needs to be done, but I'm not going to fall apart over this. Okay?"

The relief that washed through me told me how terrified I had been of just that. I nodded again. "Okay. But I'd still like to come. If you write me a note, I can talk to my teachers today and bring work along with me. Is leaving tomorrow soon enough?"

"Yes, sure. It's not like he's going anywhere." She clapped a hand over her mouth. "Oh! What an awful thing to say."

But I grinned at her, glad beyond words to see her able to make a little joke. That, more than her assurances, convinced me she wasn't about to revisit Zombie Mom. "Grampa wouldn't mind. Remember those terrible jokes he used to tell?"

## JACK

"Yeah, of course you have to go. He's your grandfather." I said the words and tried to mean them.

"It'll only be a few days," Lucy said. "Though I guess we might have to go back for the funeral or something."

"No worries—I still have over three weeks till my next scheduled appointment." I meant it to sound jokey, but it came out pretty tense. Three weeks sounded like a lot less than a month.

"I know. I was thinking though—can you come over tonight?"

"Why, yes, I can." I leaned over and gave her a smooch on the neck, and then another, and then nibbled the row of rings in her ear, breathing in a combination of smells: shampoo and fresh air and exhaust from the school bus parked beside us. "We definitely need a proper goodbye."

She snuggled in against me for a delicious moment, then straightened up and frowned at me. "I have more than that in mind. Work first. Then play."

The bus was about to leave. I grabbed one more kiss, then hopped on.

Lucy had cleared off the living-room coffee table, covered it with a cloth and put an odd assortment of items on it: a candle and matches, a large saucepan, a plastic milk pitcher...

Looking equal parts solemn and embarrassed, she said, "I thought we could do a thing I read about before I go. It might help."

"A thing?"

She squirmed a bit. "You know, a spell, I guess. I seem to have trouble acknowledging the craziness of what we're doing."

"No shit. Okay, I'm in." I was way past protesting that I didn't believe in magic. At this point, belief didn't even seem relevant. I'd thought seriously about going into the Catholic church in my neighborhood to ask about exorcism—and not only was I not Catholic, I'd only ever been in a church once, for my cousin's wedding. My parents could be transported by the wonders of fish-scale structure or the miracle of birth, but they didn't have a religious bone between them.

So there I was, sitting on the floor at the coffee table, watching Lucy melt a bit of wax, stick the candle on the bottom of the pot and pour in water from the pitcher. Then she sat back.

"So…here's how it works. If it works. It's all about focused intent and channeling energy. We light the candle. You watch it burn, imagining that the candle flame is the spell that's binding you. When the candle burns down to the water, the flame goes out, and that breaks the spell."

"That's it?" It seemed a little minimal, considering the weirdness I was up against.

"It's the only one I could find that was simple enough to manage at short notice. But it's supposed to be effective." She shrugged. "At least, you know, according to witch.com."

Something else was bothering me. "Lucy…what if I go over there while we're watching the candle? I mean, it's happened before when I was zoning out."

"Oh. God. I never thought of that." We stared at each other, trying to weigh risks we didn't understand. Lucy spoke first.

"It has to be your decision, Jack. Maybe we shouldn't risk it—I mean, it's likely this won't even work."

"Theoretically, I have till the full moon."

She nodded. "I know. But whether the theory holds…" She looked at me, her face solemn. "Jack, this is going to sound kind of crazy. But I have this feeling like we're in a triangle—that you are being pulled by the Match Girl, and somehow I'm her counterpart, pulling you back."

I thought about that—or, rather, didn't *think* so much as tried to picture it. "That seems right somehow. Though it's not what I want our relationship to be about."

She gave the little smile, an almost secret little smile, which put all kinds of distracting ideas in my head, but she stayed on topic.

"If you want to try this, let's hold hands while we do it. You think about the candle and the spell. I'll think about keeping you here."

And that's what we did. I'll admit I was nervous, and glad to feel Lucy's strong little hands firmly squeezing mine. It all seemed so silly, like something thirteen-year-old girls would do at a sleepover, and yet it was deadly serious.

Lucy lit the candle, and at first I was restless, my mind flitting everywhere and not wanting to light on the wavery little flame. But gradually it drew me in, and I felt my focus become narrow and steady. And then I pictured the Match Girl and her stupid doll, whatever she was doing with it, and layered that onto the flame.

And then…shit, I could feel it—I'm not kidding here. It was like a thousand sticky spiderwebs pulling and tugging at me. I panicked and tried to blink or look away, but I couldn't. I was just staring and staring and feeling more and more *stretched*. But I could also feel Lucy's hands, and they didn't feel like spiderwebs—they felt solid and warm. It was so weird; I could feel the pull of the binding spell getting stronger and stronger, but I could feel Lucy too, like an anchor.

And then there was a hiss, and the flame guttered and went out. And it was as if the spiderweb lines all snapped at the same moment.

I let out a long, shaky breath.

Lucy was peering at me, her eyebrows raised into question marks. "Okay?"

I nodded. "Yeah. And Lucy—I think it worked."

She jumped up and started bustling around. "Good. Then let's clear this creepy shit away and get on with a proper goodbye." She gathered up everything while I sat there, kind of in a daze, and then she took another look at me. "Jack, maybe you better test while I do this. You look a little weird."

She was right, of course. I was racy with adrenaline and probably looked stunned. Anytime I felt that weird, blood sugar could be involved.

Not only was I not low, but I was up to 12, probably from the stress. I keyed in a correction and followed Lucy into the kitchen for a glass of water *(feed a low, dilute a high)*. I resolved to put the Match Girl out of my head, at least for tonight, and focus on Lucy.

# SEVENTEEN

## KLARA

What has happened? I don't understand it, and it makes me angry. It was working, I am sure of it. Over and over, I would pull out my little Jack and concentrate fiercely on the real Jack, murmuring my spell: *"Bring Jack to me, forever to be."* It's not fancy poetry, I know, but I don't suppose Mad Gerda's spells were either. And I could feel Jack coming closer. At first it was so faint I thought it was just my own hopeful imagining. But it grew stronger each time I repeated the spell. And then suddenly—he was gone.

Something—or someone—has interfered. But Jack is mine. He came to me, didn't he? I'm not about to let anybody else steal him away.

My spell worked the first time. It was slow, but it was working. I'll just start again. I have plenty of time, after all. I will never give up—and sooner or later, Jack will come to me before that interfering nosybody can get in my way.

# EIGHTEEN

## LUCY

It was so strange and sad to walk into Grampa's house and know he'd never set foot in there again. But there was too much to do to think about it for long. Mom had a long conversation with Uncle Steve on the phone, which sounded at my end like this: "Oh, good. I'm so glad you can get away. Saturday? What time? We'll meet your train. Meanwhile...yes, okay...Do you have any preferences? Okay, well, we can try. Lucy and I will get things started...What? Oh God, Stephen, I don't know. We'll talk about it when you get here."

"What?" I asked.

"Hmm?" My mom seemed deep in thought, or maybe submerged in panic.

"Oh God, what?"

"Oh. Shamus made both Stephen and me executors, just to cover the bases. But Stephen's asking if I'll do it all and take some money for it."

"What's an executor?"

She shook her head, looking tired. "It's the person who carries out the instructions in a person's will—takes care of all the financial stuff, sells the house, finds out what other money there is, doles it all out the way the will specifies. It's a lot of trouble and time, is what it is. Meanwhile, it's Thursday and he wants to have the service on Sunday or Monday, so he can get back."

So we launched into it—arranging cremation, tracking down Grampa's church and setting a service date with the priest, writing an obituary, going through his phone list to find and call his friends, tracking down cousins and aunties I'd barely heard of, ordering flowers. In between all that, we tackled the fridge, throwing out the old festering food. Then we brought in some basics for ourselves.

"God, Mom," I finally blurted out. "Did you have to do all this when Dad died?" It was only Friday night, and I was exhausted. Trying to sleep on Grampa's lumpy old couch the night before hadn't helped.

She sighed and shook her head. "It's pretty much a blur," she said. "But I remember feeling like I couldn't handle doing one more thing, yet dreading when it would be done and reality would well and truly hit." It was the most she'd ever told me about that time, and I had a sudden urge to jump up and hug her—hard. But I hesitated and lost my chance. Mom glanced at the clock on the kitchen wall and jumped up. "Oh Lord, I have to meet with that priest soon. Lucy, would you be a dear and rustle up some sort of lunch? And then you can stay here, if you want, and get some homework done."

"You sure?" I was grateful for a break, though the worry about my mom was not banished yet. But she gave me a quick squeeze and said that it was great having me here, but yes, she was fine.

～❦～

I didn't get much work done. Mostly I wandered around Grampa's house, looking at his stuff and remembering him. He teased me about how I looked when we started visiting last year. Mom resolutely never commented on my new style, and Kate asked me earnest questions like, "Who are you armoring yourself against?" But Grampa took one look at me and cackled, "Well, Little Miss Hole-in-Your-Stockings, did you get in a fight with a pair of scissors?" And then he ran his gnarled old hand over my chopped and razored hair. He saw me just fine through the hair dye and boots, and I loved him for that.

I found a stack of photo albums in the shelf beside his easy chair, full of pictures of my dad and Uncle Steve as kids. I looked carefully at the photos of my grandmother. According to family lore, she had waited dutifully until her sons went off to university, then packed her bags and left, eventually landing in California and remarrying. She had written to my dad every Christmas, but never came to visit.

I put the albums on the coffee table, thinking Uncle Steve might want to look through them. He'd told Mom he just wanted to get rid of the house and its contents as quickly as possible, and we should take anything we wanted as a keepsake. I wandered aimlessly around, glancing into kitchen cupboards and at the cheap old knickknacks on the shelves, and then I opened the door to the dark, ladder-like steps leading up to the attic. I had a sudden, vivid memory of discovering these stairs as a kid and being firmly forbidden to go up there. "It's not safe, Lucy," my dad had said as he latched the little hook that locked the door.

There was a light switch on the wall, and when I flipped it, a dim light blinked on. Still, I rummaged around in the kitchen until I found a flashlight—and then headed up.

~ ⁊ ~

Mom got back late in the afternoon with a liquor-store bag, from which she unpacked two bottles of wine. One went into the fridge, and the other she opened. To my surprise she poured two glasses, handed one to me and sprawled out in Grampa's big armchair, easing off her shoes.

"Time for a break." She sighed and then lifted her glass to me. "Here's to your Grampa Shamus."

I reached over to clink her glass, and we had a solemn sip. "I hope Stephen appreciates this." Mom sighed again.

"How are we doing?" I asked.

"I think things are pretty much ready to go. If Stephen wants to change anything about the service, he can see to it on Saturday, but he doesn't seem to care." She leaned her head back against the headrest, which honestly looked kinda grubby, and closed her eyes. "Let's find somewhere nice to go for dinner tonight. I'm tired of camping here."

We sat in silence for a bit—a nice silence, though, not awkward. Things seemed to be changing with my mom and me. When I thought about it, maybe they had been for a while, but this trip was pushing things along. I didn't feel like we were on eggshells with each other anymore. Mom sat up, and her eyes fell on the photo albums. "What're these?"

"I found them this afternoon. I thought Uncle Stephen might want to take a look."

She picked one up and sat beside me on the couch. "We should take a look too." She took a good slug of wine, as if to fortify herself, and opened the album.

What happened next was amazing, but it's hard to explain why. It sounds normal, right? Looking at family photos after someone dies. But for us, it wasn't normal. We laughed over goofy photos of my dad as a kid, his hair so blond I could hardly believe it was him. We watched him grow tall and skinny and pimply and then turn into a handsome, dark-haired college student. When we hit the wedding photos, my mom started bawling, and so did I, and she put her arm around me and passed the Kleenex box, and we sniveled our way through my mom showing off her pregnant belly and my dad holding a red-faced bundle that was allegedly me and then me as a toddler on this same old couch. And then my mom closed the album firmly, dragged her hand across her nose and said, "That's all I can handle for now." She looked at me and I saw her lip kind of quiver, and she said, "But this was good. And I'm really glad you're here with me." And then I got teary again too, but we laughed it off and jumped up to get ready for dinner.

On the way to the restaurant, I sent Jack a quick text. **Miss you. But I think I have my mom back!**

⁓♾⁓

Over dinner I told Mom about my find in the attic. "It's mostly junk, I guess, beat-up old chairs, bags of clothes or curtains or whatever, some suitcases like the kind you see in old movies. I found a box of books with leather bindings that looked intriguing, but it turned out to be a set called *Reader's Digest Condensed Books*. They're, like, four famous books per volume, each down to 100 pages."

Mom snorted in amusement. "Great literature for the short attention span."

I hurried on. "But anyway, *under* that box I found an old metal trunk. It's not big, but it's kinda heavy to bring down the stairs myself. I dragged it out into the open, but I couldn't get the lid up. I don't think it's locked, just all rusted and jammed."

"Huh. I think your grampa would have been too young to be in the war," said Mom thoughtfully, "but maybe it's some other kind of travel trunk?"

"It seems too small for that," I said.

"Curiouser and curiouser!" Mom's eyes widened. "You don't suppose he was carrying on a secret love affair and that's why his wife left? Maybe we shouldn't open it."

"You're kidding, right? We have to open it."

That night we rummaged around in Grampa's basement until we found WD-40, pliers and a screwdriver, and then we climbed up to the attic and pried open the trunk's clasp. The lid lifted with a screech, and I peered in.

"If a mouse jumps out of here, I'm going to scream," I said as I cautiously lifted out a small, moth-eaten blanket.

"That looks like a baby blanket." My mom sounded bemused. "But it's such coarse wool, too scratchy for a baby."

Next came some brittle folded papers that I opened gently and trained the flashlight on. One seemed to be a United States immigration record for Donal and Sigrid Sullivan, dated 1811. The other was a marriage license, dated Boston 1812, between Donal Sullivan and Sigrid Larsdatter. Oh, that was cool. "Mom, that must be a Sullivan ancestor. Geez, how many greats back would that be?" Under the certificate was a folded piece of lace, now yellow and stiff.

"Marriage veil?" My mom guessed. "Though…" She peered at the two papers. "They came over as a married couple. Why would they get married again?"

Finally, at the very bottom of the chest, I found the real treasure: a sheaf of papers, punched and tied together between cardboard ends, inscribed on the first page: *Sigrid's Story: as told to her daughter-in-law Anna Sullivan (née Mahoney) on June 12, 1859.* Gently I turned a few pages. Lines of slanted, loopy handwriting in faded black ink stared back at me. I shook my head, frustrated by the dim light. "Let's have a closer look downstairs."

"You check it out, luv. I'm done like dinner."

*Luv.* Both my parents used to call me that when I was little—but I hadn't heard it in ages. It sounded nice.

"Sleep well," I said. "Mom—Uncle Steve said I could choose something as a keepsake. Do you think I could have this?"

"You can ask him," she said. "Something that old might be worth something, I suppose, but I doubt Stephen cares." She yawned hugely as we started down the stairs. "Lucy, are you okay on that couch really?"

"I'm getting used to it," I lied.

"Maybe we should get a hotel room for tomorrow," she said. "The little guest bed's pretty bad too, and I just can't bring myself to sleep in Shamus's bed."

No. Me neither.

## JACK

With Lucy gone, the Match Girl weighed more heavily on my mind. Now that I'd discovered the pattern, it was impossible to tell myself these were isolated freak events that would likely never happen again. The next full moon seemed to be racing toward me. I thought more than once about telling my parents—even headed down the stairs from my room once to do it—but in the end I just couldn't find the words. *Hey, guys, you won't believe what's been happening.* No, they wouldn't. And I would have found that easier to take when this first started, back when I didn't really believe it either. Now, I didn't want to waste time with medical tests or shrinks or "proving" to my parents that this was somehow real. I just wanted them to help me make it stop.

Rather than do nothing, I continued to slog through the Andersen books, though I was sick of them—and him. At least they helped me fall asleep at night: I'd hardly ever read anything more boring.

It was getting close to midnight, and I was just about to chuck HCA's diary and turn out the light when my eye caught something that chased away all thoughts of sleep. In the middle of a long entry about a trip to Italy, I saw *the young girl who used to sell matches outside the theater.* My heart started tripping fast as I stared at the words. I scanned back to find the place where the passage started and read more carefully:

There are beggars on the streets everywhere; they are quite a nuisance and my landlady warned me that many are also accomplished pickpockets so one must avoid any close contact. Strange how one beggar can stir one's sympathy, but many become menacing. But there was one little waif, clutching a tray of grimy trinkets, who caught my attention. She jogged a memory, but it was some time before I realized whom she reminded me of: the young girl who used to sell matches outside the theater...

I was just a boy myself, new to the city and poor as a church mouse, struggling to survive on the pittance the Royal Danish Theater paid me as a choirboy. But the little girl —she could not have been more than ten years of age—who stood on the street with her matches until the last patron and player left the theater was clearly worse off than I. She was there on the coldest nights, shivering in her thin shawl, and though I had no spare coins for her I did sometimes slip an extra piece of bread or a hard-boiled egg from my aunt's table into my coat pocket to give her. Then one night the street was empty of vendors, and when I mentioned it one of the players told me the police had cleared them off due to complaints from the theater patrons.

I was still living at my aunt's, for though the realization that she was effectively running a brothel shamed me intolerably, for the present I had no other recourse. And I thought no more about the match girl until one night when I was returning "home" unusually late, and saw a slim figure ahead of me. Hearing my footsteps, she glanced back fearfully, giving me a glimpse of her. I recognized her at once, the very striking large blue eyes in a wan little face, and waved to reassure her, but it seemed to have the opposite effect. She redoubled her steps, hurrying to a hovel at the end of the street and slipping in the door.

I didn't like to speak unnecessarily to my aunt, but I could not resist asking her about the girl the next day. She's an inveterate gossip who goes out of her way to learn her neighbors' business.

"Oh, that's a sad tale," she told me. "That's Sigrid Larsdatter's child. They say she ran off with a foreign sailor, leaving her daughter and husband behind."

I was shocked. "How could she do such a thing?"

"Oh well." My aunt shrugged. Her morals, needless to say, were sorely lacking. "I don't blame her one whit for leaving that Henricksen. He was always a mean old drunk, that one, and I've no doubt her life with him was a misery. But leaving the child—that's harsh.

"Seems to me the baby was with her grandparents for some time," she mused. "Yes, that's right. Then the grandmother died, and the child was sent back to her father. But Henricksen has gone from bad to worse since then. He's not fit to raise a goat."

I thought about that young girl sometimes, though I rarely ever caught a glimpse of her after that. Soon I was able to move to a more respectable lodging, and I forgot about the girl until some time later, when my aunt sent me a note to say she'd been found dead and frozen in the street.

I was young enough to be shocked by her end, horrified even, and full of raging indignation against a world that would stand indifferent to a poor child's suffering. And I took up my pen. Do you know, I had forgotten that altogether until now! I wrote the girl's history in a lather, more a fiery sermon than a story, with no thought but to find an outlet for my turmoil. I wonder if I still have it among my papers?

Imagine, that was almost twenty years ago. I find that child's plight still moves me; perhaps I shall find my old account and see if it can't be turned into a proper tale.

It is too hot here to write seriously. How anything gets accomplished in this scorching sun is beyond me; I find I must lie down each afternoon just to keep from fainting and my face is as red as a lobster. If I ever return here, it must be in the cooler season...

The Match Girl was real. I could hardly believe it. My brain was spinning, trying to grasp what it meant. We were dealing with a "real" ghost, not a fictional character? Was that better or worse?

I grabbed my phone to call Lucy, then glanced at the time. Twelve thirty. Damn. I thought she said they were staying at her grandfather's house, not a hotel, but I didn't know if she had her own room. Lucy wouldn't mind being woken up for this, but her mom would. Reluctantly, I turned out the light. It felt like morning would never come.

I barely slept all night, my stupid brain rehashing Andersen's journal entry over and over. Plus, I was afraid I'd dream of Little Creepy Girl, with my brain so full of her, and that probably kept me awake too. Then I overslept, staggering into the kitchen in a fog.

"You look terrible, Jack—are you okay?" My mom kind of did a double take when she looked up from her coffee and paper.

"Yeah, just slept badly, and now I'm late. Is there any more of that?" I hefted the coffee pot experimentally and filled up a travel mug.

"Toast?"

"Maybe just a PB sandwich—it'll be faster and I can take it with me." I felt rather than saw her eyes on me, felt her unspoken question. "Honestly, I'm fine—just tired. I tested 6.3 this morning."

"Okay, kiddo. Just for the record—I didn't ask."

"I know." In fairness, she hadn't, and I *had* sounded a little testy. "I gotta run. Thanks for the coffee."

I didn't want to phone Lucy on the bus—too loud and public—but I texted her. **Crazy news. Call u at lunchtime?**

By second period, I realized I had messed up. I was down to one test strip, up to 16, and my set, which I should have changed that morning, was looking pretty frayed around the edges. Once the infusion set gets pulled loose or just overstays its welcome in that patch of skin, it doesn't matter how much insulin you shoot in there; it doesn't get absorbed. I wasn't going to make the biology field trip unless I got it all sorted at lunchtime. Reluctantly, I called my mom.

"Um, hi. I wondered if you'd be free to bring me some stuff."

"What stuff?"

"I need test strips and a new set. I can grab the bus if you can't come, but there's this biology trip to the Turtle Trauma Centre and…"

"I can come right at noon—is that soon enough?"

"Yeah, I'll be waiting at the door. Thanks, Mom."

"You're not done with me yet. I know you were tired this morning, but Jack, I won't always be around to bring you stuff."

*Oh, here we go.* "I know. Look, I'm sorry."

She just kept on like I hadn't said anything. My dad calls it her "Danish implacability."

"So your backup supplies are going to be really important…"

"Right. Look, I have to get back—"

"…which is why I suggested you keep extra supplies in your locker."

# NINETEEN

## LUCY

I took the notebook to bed with me. Uncle Steve was arriving by train from Montreal the next morning, and I wanted to know what I had found before asking for it. First, though, I wanted to call Jack—I hadn't heard from him or even checked Facebook all day. But when I dug my phone out of my purse, the battery was dead. *Now* I remembered the low battery signal I'd vaguely registered the night before. With a muttered curse, I looked around the cluttered room for a free wall outlet. Grampa's outlets all seemed to be hidden behind immovable furniture. I had to haul the couch out from the wall and fold myself over the back to plug in my phone. Then I settled into the Couch of Pain.

It was hard to make out the handwriting at first, but once I got used to it, I read quickly. Sigrid's voice became clearer and clearer, until I almost forgot I was reading.

It was like I was meeting an ancestor I never knew existed, seeing her life through her eyes.

I was born Sigrid Larsdatter. Now I am Sigrid Sullivan. I know my life draws to a close, and I wish to tell of those things I was never able to speak of—the secret sorrow and shame that has been the dark and constant witness to the blessings I found in this New World. Reason tells me that my Klara will never set eyes on this record, yet my heart does hold the stubborn hope that one day she may, and know that her mother, though failing to provide for her, did not part from her willingly or fail to love her to the end of her days. For I am mother to more than the four I bore in America. This is my story.

"Sigrid, clear these little ones out of my way." My mother pushed back the hair that had escaped her kerchief and shooed the two youngest children as though they were chickens. I ran to scoop up the baby and grab Hanne's hand, leading them away from the hearth where Mama wrestled with the heavy soup pot. Then she put it down abruptly and hurried to the night jar, vomiting into it.

I sighed. Pregnant again. That would make six, and only Johan, my older brother, earning his own keep. No wonder the furrow between her brows had appeared so often of late.

My father arrived home late, black from the coal he shoveled all day, drawn with weariness. He didn't complain about the thin soup my sister Greta set before him, but tore into it, carefully mopping up the last drops with his bread.

"Did you get paid today?" Mama asked, once he had done.

He nodded. "Most of it."

We all let out breath we hadn't realized we were holding: there would be better food tomorrow, not the gruel that sometimes kept us going when his customers showed empty pockets on their due day.

I heard my parents' low voices that night, my father's voice rising once in anger—as though my mother had conceived by her own willful design, and he'd played no part in it.

Only a few days later my father told me he had found me a position at the Black Horse Inn, where he delivered the coal. It was his habit to take a drink there when he'd had a good pay—a small enough reward, and even that more than we could afford.

I was nearly fifteen years old, and I thought I was used to hard work—but my first day in the laundry showed me the difference between the up-and-down work in a family household and ten relentless hours doing the same backbreaking task over and over. By midday my back and arm muscles were screaming for a rest, and I was drenched in my own sweat, from the heat of the fires and the clouds of steam that enveloped us as we hooked out the sheets, towels and kitchen cloths from huge tubs of hot water. The soapy linens were dunked into cold rinse water, then fed through a mangle that took all my strength to turn and would flatten your arm up to the shoulder as happily as a sheet if you weren't careful. Then the next batch went into the suds to boil as we pegged out the clean laundry.

"Lucky for us, this ain't a proper fancy hotel," said Frau Olsdatter. She was in charge of the laundry, and while she put me to work smartly, she was kind enough and didn't stint on her share. "Then we'd have to scrub out every stain on a washboard. But Herr Jensen don't care if the sheets is a bit spotty." Herr Jensen was the manager, a balding, paunchy man in a frock coat who'd glanced up at me from his ledger when I presented myself that morning, said, "Come with me" and led me to the laundry without another word.

I went home that night with a new understanding of my father's heavy footfall. Barely able to eat or answer my mother's questions, I crawled early to my bed. The next morning I was so sore I had to bite back tears as I dressed myself. My mother looked at me with sharp concern but bit her lip and said nothing.

"It will be fine," I mumbled. "Laundry is just twice a week, so today will be easier." I dreaded going back, but I knew the family depended on me.

That day I found myself in the hotel kitchen, scrubbing pots, stacking plates, emptying overflowing garbage bins and sweeping and mopping the floors, which seemed to be constantly coated with grease, crumbs and peelings. Wednesday I was put to work sweeping and mopping the long halls and stairways of the inn, and cleaning out the ashes from every fireplace. This last required going into the guests' rooms, which frighted me some. But I went with a chambermaid named Elsa, a cheerful girl who showed me how to knock and call out before entering the room. In the time it took me to sweep the ashes into a bucket, dump it out into the ash bin at the end of the hall and tidy up the mess around the grate, she'd stripped and made up the bed and gathered up any trash left by the last guest. Then I took the garbage and linens away while she swept the room. The worst job was cleaning the privies, which Elsa showed me how to do but didn't help with, saying, "I did my share of that when I started here."

Thursday was laundry again, and Frau Olsdatter grinned when she saw me. "Still here? Good for you." She already had two of the big kettles filled with water and was working on a third, her thick red arms hoisting buckets tirelessly. "Here, grab a bucket."

"We always start girls on laundry day," she told me later. "Why is that?" I asked, since Frau Olsdatter seemed to be waiting for it. We had taken our midday meal to a little area behind the hotel where servants were allowed. It was shaded by the building, and the alleyway behind allowed a little breeze to reach us, affording some relief from the inferno of the laundry. My new position didn't pay much, but it included a daily meal, which, as Elsa had said, wasn't always good but at least was filling.

"Them as aren't prepared to work hard don't come back," she said. "They wake up with everything hurting and give it up. Plus, you can't shirk here, 'cause I'm always at your side."

The work got easier as I became accustomed to it, and before the month was out, even the laundry days didn't leave me as sore and scuttled. I can't say I learned to enjoy it, but I liked the companionship of Frau Olsdatter and Elsa. When I brought home my first pay, my father counted it carefully and gave two of the eight coins back to me. "For your own necessaries," he said and gave me a brief smile that was somehow painful. I thought on that smile in bed that night, and it came to me that he was ashamed to have to send me out to work and then take my earnings.

I'd been at the inn about six months when Elsa got herself married to a shopkeeper and left her position, and I was given the job of chambermaid. Though I had worked mainly in the empty rooms after guests left, I'd had an eyeful by then of some of the rough characters who stayed in that inn, and heard Elsa's stories of all her tricks and strategies for staying out of the way of the drunk or lecherous ones. And I'd changed a lot in those few months. Before, I would have shrunk at the thought of fending off a man or going into a room where a pleasure lady did her business. I was more confident now—and strong from my time in the laundry. But I never told my parents about the goings-on in some of those rooms.

One morning I was carrying a stack of clean sheets down the hall to the big cupboard where they were stored when I paused outside a door. The most delightful sound was seeping through—a trilling like birdsong, only sorted into the liveliest, happiest tune. I had to stay and listen, it made me smile so. For a stolen moment, I forgot the gritty floors and worries at home.

A few days later I was sent to change the sheets in that same room. "Is he out?" I asked, hoping to work unobserved.

Herr Jensen shook his head. "That one's never out—he's laid up with his leg in a splint." I must have stood there a second too long, because his lips pursed with irritation and he flapped his hand at me. "Get on then, girl! Smartly!"

And that's when I first laid eyes on Donal Sullivan.

He was sitting up in the bed, with his bandaged leg propped on a cushion. But that's not what I saw. I saw a young, open face, with curly dark hair and eyes green as a cat's. He smiled a welcome at me, and I felt the blood rush into my face. I normally avoided eye contact with guests, but I couldn't look away. Or perhaps I could—but I didn't want to!

Tongue-tied, I gestured with my stack of sheets, and he reached for the crutch leaning against the bed. It was laborious work to ease himself over to the edge, and the whole time I just stood there, not knowing what to say. But then, as he went to stand up, he grimaced and looked back at me.

"Help, please?"

He wasn't Danish, that was clear. But his request was plain enough, and shy though I was, there was nothing for it but to run over and grab his arm. I helped him hobble to the armchair that had been brought up for him, settled his bad leg on the footstool and then set to work.

The first trills made me stop.

"Is it all right?" he asked, gesturing at the small metal flute—not much more than a whistle, really.

I smiled. "Yes, please."

So he whistled while I worked, and somehow that put me right at ease. By the time I was done, I didn't hesitate at all to offer to help him back to the bed, but he shook his head.

"I stay here some." Another smile. "Sorry—my Danish is small."

"Where are you from?" The words came out of me before I could stop them.

"Ireland. I am a sailor."

"What happened to your leg?" I pointed, in case he didn't understand.

Another grimace, and he mimed snapping a stick. "A storm." He shrugged with a rueful look. "Now I am on land for long time."

"Your music is lovely." I couldn't believe my own cheek. I never spoke with customers this way. But there was something about this young man that drew me in.

He was there for three months all told, and by the time he set sail again I wasn't even finding excuses to visit his room—I was sneaking in every chance I got. I loved him madly; that's the long and short of it. He was merry and quick to laugh, so unlike my own stern father, and he made me feel—oh, like some rare and lovely creature. Donal's Danish became better and better, thanks to me, and on the day he got his splint removed and his leg pronounced sound, he asked me to marry him. Though there was more to it than that: "Will you marry me, Sigrid, and come with me to America?" He said the New World was a place where a young couple could make a good life. With work on a trans-Atlantic ship, he would make enough from two crossings to book my passage.

*America.* The very sound of the word was foreign and frightening. But Donal was right when he said we would never be anything but lowly in Copenhagen. And he gave me courage.

There wasn't much fuss about it. I said yes, and he promised to come for me as soon as he could.

But first would come the leaving, and vast ocean voyages, the distances beyond my imagining. We had just two more weeks while Donal built up the strength in his leg, and the thought of parting made me reckless, I suppose. We became lovers, and although it was furtive and hurried, our first time was the sweetest day of my short life. That night I lay awake, for once not minding the baby's cries or my sisters' squirmy bodies pressing me to the edge of the bed—just holding the happiness of it to my heart.

And then he was gone.

~ ∘⌒ ~

I recognized the early signs. Hadn't I seen them often enough with my mother? But I managed to hide them. And of course I was scared—I was facing so many unknowns already, and here was one more, before I was ready. But I wasn't terrified or despairing, because I knew my Donal was coming for me. It never crossed my mind that I could be ruined.

The mean streets of Copenhagen were littered with them, the unwed girls who'd borne babies and been cast off like rubbish. They sold themselves for a few coins or some food, sometimes with their children clinging to their skirts. The children were dirty and pale, with the drawn look of illness stamped on their little faces. I remember passing one of these women with my mother on the way to market once. Her little boy's hair was thin and patchy, mottled with bald spots, and I asked Mama what was wrong with him. She glanced askance, as though he were some malignant growth sprouted from the ground.

"Don't look at them," she hissed, and yanked on my hand to keep me trotting. "There's nothing can be done."

But that would not be my fate. It was not so unusual for babies to be born a few months after the wedding. My Donal was coming for me, and if he found good ships and fair weather, with a month for each crossing he might be back before anyone noticed my condition. I did not let myself think of the perils that lay between his leaving and our reunion.

I was about four months gone, expecting news of Donal any day, when my mother's eyes proved too sharp for me. "Sigrid, reach up and get me that crock of lard," she said. It was my day off, and we were making the pasties my papa took to work for his supper. I heard the hissing intake of her breath as I stretched toward the shelf. Ever thrifty, Mama waited until I had safely settled the crock on the table. As I turned, she slapped my face so hard I felt the imprint of her hand burn my skin like a brand.

"*Slut.*" When I risked a glance, her face was a mask of fury. Then it contorted, and she sank into a chair, her face in her hands. "You stupid girl. What have you gone and done?" I heard the fear in her voice, and that was worse than her anger.

I knelt beside her. "Mama, it's all right. I will be married soon—I won't shame you."

"You have already shamed me." Still, I saw hope flare in her eyes. "So. This man—this man you have taken up with without our knowledge or say-so—will marry you. Who is he then?"

I began to tell her about Donal, and her mouth puckered up with bitterness. "A foreigner—and a sailor! Could you be any dimmer! And where is he now, this *sailor*?" The word spat out, as though Donal were a cutthroat or thief.

"He is working to earn—"

"He has sailed away, you mean, leaving you here, full of his baby!"

"He will come back for me. Soon now."

"Did I raise you to be an idiot?"

"Mama, no. He wants to marry me. He *will* come for me. We are going to America."

That earned me another slap, though this one was halfhearted. "America. Did he give you a written vow? Are there witnesses? Do you even know where he lives?"

I stared at her. "No, Mama. Why would I need such things?"

Her shoulders slumped. "You have nothing, girl. Nothing. Every destitute woman on the street has been told the same tale."

Tears stung my eyes. "Donal will be true to me— you'll see!"

Mama tightened her mouth even further and said nothing, just heaved herself up from the chair and went back to her work.

# TWENTY

## LUCY

I was so caught up in Sigrid's story that I jumped at the ping announcing a text. Feeling a little disoriented— like, *What am I doing here in the twenty-first century?*— I bent over the couch and groped at the phone where it was tethered to the wall outlet. Jack's text read **r u still up?** All wrapped up in Sigrid's love story, I felt a wave of longing for Jack. My battery reading was a measly 14 percent, but it would do for a short call. I pulled the phone out of the charger and dialed.

## JACK

It was so great to hear Lucy's voice. I was kind of embarrassed at how strongly I reacted, actually. I mean, it wasn't like she'd been gone a month or anything. And to my surprise, she sounded all excited about something.

"Jack, you'll never guess what I found at my grampa's."

"Um…a skeleton in the closet?" Too late it occurred to me that this was a horrible thing to say when someone has actually died. But Lucy just rattled on.

"You're surprisingly close. I found this old journal, kind of—well, it's the story of my great-great—God knows how many *great*—grandmother. It's this incredible account of how she fell in love with an Irish sailor and went to America. And Jack, she was Danish. Her name was Sigrid—wait, let me check—yeah, Sigrid Larsdatter."

I confess I'd zoned out a bit, not being that fascinated by some dusty old family history, but that name jolted me right into a hyperalertness that was almost painful. I actually felt like my brain was *buzzing*, madly trying to connect these wild dots.

"Lucy, stop."

There was dead silence on the line. Then, quietly and a bit ominously, like *you'd better have a good reason to have been so rude*: "What?"

"Sigrid Larsdatter? Seriously, that was her name?"

"Yes. Jack, what's this about? I could hardly make up a name like that."

"No, it's just…sorry, my mind is kind of exploding here. Just wait, okay? I have something important to read to you."

When I'd finished reading the passage from Andersen, neither of us could speak for a while. The silence stretched out between us as we tried to take in the implications. Then Lucy plunged in.

"So…the Match Girl was Sigrid's daughter, and Sigrid was my direct ancestor. And Sigrid went to America and left the little girl behind? Dear God."

There was a tinny *beep* and a surprising vicious expletive from Lucy. "Jack, I have hardly any battery. I have to go and finish reading this. I'll call tomorrow…"

Her voice disappeared into crackling and a dial tone, but I thought I caught the words "love you" before it died out for good.

I was afraid my father would beat me, but he did not even say one word about it. The only way I knew my mother had told him was that when I arrived back from work a few days later, he did not greet me or even look at me. He acted like I did not exist all evening, and at first I was relieved. After all, my father and I already saw each other little and spoke less. But you've no idea how painful being invisible eventually becomes.

When a week had gone by and no more was said, I thought I had seen the worst of it. I would continue to work, save what I could of the few coins I had of my own, endure my father's silence and my mother's hard looks, and wait for Donal. I could not have been more wrong.

"Sit down, Sigrid, your father has news." I had barely stepped in the door when my mother hustled me to the table. I looked from one to the other, trying to read their moods. Certainly my mother seemed to have lost some of the grim bitterness she had been carrying all week. My father looked like he always did after work—tired and dirty.

"I have found you a match," he said. "You will marry Iver Henricksen ten days from today. He is widowed with no children, so he will accept the child."

"I *have* a match!" Though I had never raised my voice to my father, I was all but shrieking now. I could hardly hear myself, my head shrilled so with panic. "I am marrying Donal Sullivan, and we are going to America!"

The table jumped with the weight of my father's fist. He stood, eyes blazing, his lips pulled back in a sneer, and pointed a thick finger at me. "*You* are just another girl with a baby in her belly from a foreign sailor who found some sport on his layover. You think anyone will take you once you're fat with another man's brat?"

I was on my feet now too, half ready to run blindly out the door. "Mama!" I was crying, hating myself for it because I needed to make them understand. "Please! I can't…I *must* marry Donal! I'll die if I don't!" Stupid thing to say.

It was like begging water from stone. My mama turned cold eyes on me. "You want to talk about dying, girl? How long do you think you'll last with the street filth?" When she pushed back her chair and rose heavily to her feet, it wasn't to join in the shouting but to end it. "Your father has saved you. You will obey him, and be grateful." Then she turned her back and busied herself at the hearth, her own belly so big with child that she had to stand sideways to the stove.

My father lumbered over to his bed and eased off his big boots. "Here, Hans, can you take these for your papa?" he said. "Greta, go help your mother with the dinner." Once again, I had ceased to exist.

~∾~

I lay rigid in my bed all night, my mind racing but arriving nowhere, filled with defiance that had no outlet and, on its heels, a mounting fear. At work, exhausted though I was, there was no end to it, my brain scurrying round and round the same useless plans. I would leave my family and live on my own wages. (Yet I would be fired as soon as my condition became obvious.) I would run away. (Where?) I would send a message to Donal, and he would come for me. (How?) I would steal the passage money and go to America on my own and… (And what? Starve in a strange land?)

I had not thought my father a man to force his daughter to marry, but he believed he was saving me from far worse. A potent mix of love, shame and anger fueled him against me. Yet my mind still fixated on escape. I could not believe it would come to actually marrying Henricksen—a laborer known for his angry temper and hard drinking, a man nearly as old as my own father. A man who would bring me misery, even if I hadn't loved another.

When I arrived home from the inn that day, my mother was in labor. It went hard, leaving her whey-faced and weak, so that I had to take off work to help Greta manage everything. And the baby—he was a scrawny thing, slow to the suck. The air was thick was unspoken worry.

The days unreeled one after the other, and all I could seem to do was watch helplessly as they flew by. I never returned to work; my father had terminated my position. I was kept busy cooking and watching over the children and tending to Mama. She was too ill to burden with pleas and arguments, and my father was rarely even at home. I prayed every night for God to send Donal back to me, but with dwindling hope, until, impossibly, there were but two days left before the so-called wedding. I'd been on a long slide to a cliff, with nothing but weeds and sticks to grasp at, and now I was pitching headlong to the edge. I clutched at my father.

Weeping, wild-eyed, I begged him, but his face was stony. Before long, seemingly unable to stand me any longer, he strode out the door. How I wished I could do the same.

"Mama!" I fell to my knees before my mother's bed, where she still rested much of the day.

"For the love of God, leave off, Sigrid." She looked at me bleakly. "We cannot keep you. Even if we wished it, there simply isn't enough to go around."

I was hauled off to the pastor to have some sense talked into me. I was made to sit in a low chair, a child's chair almost, while he pursed his lips and steepled his fingers and gazed at me coldly in silence.

"You have sinned against God." His voice boomed out in the silent, chilly room. "You have sinned against the Church, against your community. You have shamed your parents, who work hard to provide for you. You could have been a help to them in your mother's illness, and instead you add to their burden. You have conceived a child from this sin, and still your father provides. He hands out salvation to you, and you spit on it. One might think the Devil himself has claimed your heart."

Oh, he made me feel like the worst creature that ever lived. I *had* sinned with Donal and burdened my mother—no wonder God had not answered my prayers. My words dried up in my mouth, and when he asked what I had to say for myself, I could do nothing but bow my head under his accusations.

"So, then. You will give up this attachment to a man who led you into sin, and obey your father as God commands us. You will pray for forgiveness from your sin, pack up your things and prepare yourself for the life of a dutiful wife. You will come meekly to the church to marry Iver Henricksen, and be grateful for this chance at redemption."

The words were like clubs, beating me deeper and deeper into my chair, so that I didn't realize he'd risen and approached me until I felt his hand on my head. My head jerked up; he gazed down at me, his mouth quirked at the corner. Compassion or disdain? I couldn't tell.

"Go in peace, my child."

---

And so I was married in a desolate and brief ceremony, followed by a desolate and blessedly brief consummation. Afterward I lay in my strange bed, in a groove made by another wife and with the musky smell of Henricksen surrounding me, and in my mind's eye I set fire to every beautiful moment I could remember with Donal. I burned them one at a time and watched them float to the ground like flaming leaves and crumble into ash.

I can't say there were any big surprises in my new married life. Henricksen's two rooms were small, dark and grimy. For the sake of the baby—Donal's baby, I reminded myself—I did my best to set them in order. I don't suppose anything had had a good cleaning since his first wife died.

He was a hard man and not inclined to sympathy or tenderness on my account. But he was only mean when he was drinking hard. Then the least thing would provoke a violent rage.

The first time he took his fist to me, I wept all night and ran to my mother at first light. Her face fell when she saw the bruise blooming across my cheekbone, but when I fell sobbing into her arms, she stiffened and held my shoulders at arm's length. "He's your husband," she said. "You must learn to manage."

"Can I not stay awhile?" I begged.

"Better not. It will just keep you thinking that this is home. You have your own home now."

And so I did learn to manage, though Henricksen's dingy rooms would never feel like home. I kept his house and made his meals and let him have his way with me in the night. I tried to become invisible when he hit the bottle—no easy feat in a tiny place. I stopped up my tears, dabbed witch hazel on my bruises and kept my troubles to myself.

I had a hard time loving the little one inside me at first. That baby, I thought, was the cause of all my misery. If there had been no baby, I would still be at home, working at the hotel and saving for the day when Donal came for me. Instead, I had a rough old man, an ugly life and a river of sadness. But as I grew big and the baby began to tumble and squirm in my belly, my feelings changed. The baby became the bright spot of joy in the grayness of my days. He was a bit of Donal, and if nothing else, we would have each other. By the time I felt the first tightening pains that told me he would soon be born, my love was as fierce as any mother's.

I say *he* since that is how I thought. But it was a little girl I birthed. My mother came to me, bossing and bullying me through when the pains came so close together I panicked and cried out that I could not go on. Nonsense, she said briskly, of course I could go on, just as all the women before me had. And because she was my mother, I did what she said and, sure enough, before long I was grunting and straining like a big old sow, and my little Klara came howling into her grandmother's arms.

It's good that she was a girl. I'm not sure Henricksen could have swallowed giving his name to Donal's boy, whatever he promised. But he softened at the sight of the tiny girl baby, and whatever his faults, he never spoke of her father.

Klara was just starting to walk, a bright, babbling little thing with the widest blue eyes. She was my only joy, but I worried after her as well. Though Henricksen had never threatened any harm to her while she was a helpless infant in a cradle, now that she was on her feet it would be harder to keep her out of his way. If she, clumsy and heedless as little ones are, ever fell against his legs when he was full of whiskey…I could not bear to picture it.

Wrapped in these gloomy thoughts, I didn't hear the knocking at the door until it grew sharp and insistent.

My legs almost gave way when I recognized him. How could I not be laid low at the sight and by the mad welter of feelings he triggered? Impossible to hold all those feelings at once, and so what they distilled into was a kind of rage—against the world, against God himself, I suppose, for letting this cruelty happen. For, you understand, I had slowly come to accept that my parents had been right, that Donal would not come. And now, pain on top of pain, here he was, and I trapped.

"They said you are married." The voice flat, accusing. Now I took in the expression on Donal's face and saw that I was not the only angry one.

"You took too long." I flung it back at him. "My parents sold me off like old stock."

"I couldn't help it. There was a storm, a shipwreck. We were blown far into the Caribbea—" His features twisted; he too carried pain inside the anger. "Ah, Sigrid, I—" He stepped inside the threshold and carefully shut the door. "Will you not come here to me?"

He opened his arms, and, married woman though I was, I held my breath and stepped into them. And it all came back—the sweetness of our time together, the happiness I'd almost grasped. I was crying, and he smoothed back my hair and whispered, "Do you love him?"

I shook my head, unable to speak.

"Then come away with me. I have a ticket for passage on my ship in my pocket. There is a room in Boston waiting for us, a start until we can plant our feet. There is no need for us to change our plans."

Klara's shrill cry came from the back room. We both stiffened.

"There's a baby?" Donal's face was a mask I couldn't read. It wasn't joy I saw there though—that was certain. I fled to the back room and stood with the baby, freshly wakened from her nap, as my mind and heart raced. I was afraid he would be gone when I returned. I was afraid he would not want her.

But when I stood before him, holding her on my hip, and said softly, "This is Klara," his eyes widened.

"But she is…how old is she?"

"She is not quite a year. Donal, she is yours. She is the reason my parents made me marry."

It is a marvelous thing to watch a man fall in love with a child. It made me fall in love with him all over again.

He stayed over an hour, as long we dared, and when he left our plans were set. I had money for coach hire and a ticket tucked into my petticoats, and had promised to board the *Liberty* two days hence.

"Be strong, Sigrid," he said before he left. "You are my wife, and Klara is my child. Whatever the law says, we have the right of it."

And who in America could say I was not Mrs. Sullivan? No one, that's who.

# TWENTY-ONE

## KLARA

Something else is happening, something I don't like. For the longest time I had no feelings at all, and then I had feelings for Jack, and that was like a beautiful bright flower in a gray room. But now I have so many other feelings, bad feelings. It happened last night—one minute I was just standing there, as usual, and the next I was weeping, overcome with fear and grief. It passed, eventually, but the memory stays with me, and sometimes shadows of sadness shudder through me, and a kind of longing.

It must be longing for Jack. I am sick and sad without him. He must come to me.

I've had the most brilliant idea—I am quite beside myself with excitement. I was bent over Little Jack, saying my spell. I get tired of saying the same words over and over, and discouraged when he doesn't come, but I keep trying. What else is there for me to do? At least when I am working with Little Jack, it keeps away those gusts of desolation.

So, as I said, I was repeating my spell when the idea came to me. I could strengthen its power by actually tying Little Jack to me. I reached up and pulled out three strands of my own hair, wrapped them round and round Little Jack's neck and body, and carefully tied them. Oh, I felt powerful then; I could feel the strength surge up within me and wrap around Little Jack as snug and tight as the coils of hair!

I am in my spot with my matches now, but I can hardly keep still for excitement. The tingly power is still in me, making me restless and fidgety. I feel as though I truly have a body. Oh, it is a wondrous feeling, almost like being alive.

# TWENTY-TWO

## JACK

The Turtle Trauma Centre had been great; it reminded me of why I was taking all these science courses in the first place. I'm not entirely sure what I want to do with them. I think probably environmental studies rather than straight biology, like my dad, but I've also wondered about veterinary college. Now I wondered about that again, though I guess nobody really makes a living doing wildlife rehab. They made it pretty clear at the center that they were always desperately short of money.

On the way home on the bus, Ms. Chung handed out our assignments. "Due on Wednesday, people. Get it in on time, or it will count as zero on your midterm report."

Midterm? That caught my attention. I wasn't used to Ontario's semester system, and I'd been acting like I had the whole year to complete my courses. Now I realized they were more than half over—and I was starting to get behind on almost everything. I had a chem lab overdue, an upcoming math test I hadn't studied for, my research project on the evidence linking neonicotinoids and other pesticides to the collapse of bee colonies barely started... I was really only caught up in drama, and that only because we were doing group work that I felt compelled to show up for.

Plus, university applications would be coming up soon. I wasn't even sure if I wanted to go straight on to university, but I thought I'd better apply anyway. So it would be my first-semester marks they'd be looking at, and especially the science and math.

The Sunday marathon D&D game Rafe had been recruiting for went up in a wistful puff of smoke. But the prospect of spending the weekend up to my ears in school-work wasn't as depressing as you might think—honestly, it would be a relief to put the mystery of the Match Girl aside and wrestle with something more concrete. I didn't think there was much more I could learn from HCA and his annoying diaries and letters anyway.

It was just as well Lucy was away—she would be a far preferable distraction. I felt a little flash of guilt. She was probably in the same boat, thanks to me, and with less chance to catch up.

Sunday afternoon. I was well into my bee-colony report, really focusing, for a change, when out of nowhere I couldn't stop thinking about how much I missed Lucy. I felt restless and anxious and like I needed to see and hold her *right now*. I checked my phone—a little past two. Her grandfather's funeral would just be starting. A phrase came to me from *Lord of the Rings*, how Bilbo says he feels "thin and stretched"—and for the first time I really got what that meant. Then I imagined the Match Girl as Gollum, and all hope of finishing the report went out the window.

I thought of taking Snowball for a walk to try to shake off my antsy feeling and creepy thoughts. But then I decided something more extreme was required, so I left the crestfallen dog behind and went for a run. I ran till I was sweaty and out of breath and too tired to be jittery. Then I came home, chugged half a Coke to prevent a post-run low, and headed to the shower. I closed my eyes under the hottest spray I could stand and focused on Lucy. I pictured every detail I could conjure, imagined the strong feeling of her hand holding on to mine when we'd done that dopey spell-breaking thing.

By the time I stepped out of the shower, I'd lost an hour and a half out of the afternoon. But I had gotten myself steady enough to go back to the bees.

## LUCY

The weekend went by in a blur. My mom rousted me up on Saturday morning so I could help her navigate across town and over the canal to the train station. Uncle Stephen arrived with a beat-up backpack and a heavy stubble of beard. On the ride back to Grampa's, and all through lunch, he talked nonstop about the Syrian refugee camp he was working in (in Lebanon, it turned out, not Syria) and the terrible conditions they faced. Finally, my mom couldn't take it anymore.

"Stephen." She waited for her tone to sink in, and finally he wound down and blinked at her.

"Sorry. What?"

"We need to talk about your father. I've done what I can, but you're his son, and there are some things you need to deal with. The priest wants to talk with you this afternoon, for one, so he can give a proper eulogy."

Stephen sighed and rubbed his hand back and forth across the top of his head, a gesture so like my dad's, I was sure my mom's heart gave the same little lurch as mine did. "I'm sorry, Alice. Jet lag and denial—it's a bad combination." He looked around the grimy little kitchen. "Is there decent coffee to be had in this hovel? Caffeine me up, and I'll be ready to get to work."

Mom caught my eye as she put the kettle on, and we shared an internal smirk. It was a family joke how Uncle Stephen would happily live for months on end in a tent when he was on assignment, but insisted on high-end everything when he was home. It was almost worth sleeping on that gross couch to witness his horror when he realized we'd been camping at Grampa's. "You're not telling me you're *staying* here! You mean *overnight*? Good God. I'll call my hotel right away and book an extra room. On me."

We checked in en route to the cathedral, and while the two beds piled high with white duvets looked wonderful, I found I was sad to leave Grampa's. It seemed like the real goodbye, yet we'd just rushed off without a thought.

"Do you want to stay here and get some work done, Lucy?" Mom and Stephen were heading right out again.

Work. I'd barely touched it since we'd left town, and I was behind to start with. But I knew if I stayed, I wouldn't get anything done anyway, not with Sigrid's notebook waiting for me. And there was something else on my mind.

"Um, Mom…do you think I could get something to wear to the funeral? If there's anywhere nearby to shop, that is." I found it surprisingly hard to say, as if I were admitting or surrendering to something. So then I felt compelled to explain, "I just want to wear something Grampa would like."

～❧～

The next day was the funeral, and we were all fried by the time we said good night to Uncle Steve and headed back to our hotel room. He'd been pretty intense over dinner, trying to sort out enough details that he could head back to Montreal the next morning and catch a night flight to Lebanon. Mom flopped onto her bed, kicked off her shoes and groaned in relief.

"Bath and bed for me. Though I bet I won't be able to sleep."

I glanced around the room, wondering how I could read, or do anything, without disturbing her. Then I noticed the little built-in lights in the tall headboard—almost like those airplane spotlights. With them on, there'd be very little light reaching the other bed.

I should never have stopped. I should have gotten into the coach and not looked back until I was on the ship.

But to disappear with no explanation and no fare-well—how could I be so heartless? And so I pulled the coach over and knocked on my mother's door.

Her face softened at the sight of Klara. Her little Peder, never strong, had not survived the winter, and she had taken it hard. But I didn't waste time with pleasant-ries. "I've come to say goodbye. I am sailing for America with Donal."

Mama opened her mouth in protest, but before a sound came out closed it again. I could almost see her calculating, and whether she simply accepted that there was no stopping me this time or concluded that I was better off away, in the end she simply nodded. Then her eyes fell on Klara, and the dismay returned.

"But you can't be thinking of taking her?"

"Of course I am taking her. She is my child—and Donal's."

"But the crossing! It's terrible hard on the little ones. You've no idea! Many don't survive it. Oh, Sigrid, what if she should sicken and perish?" Her hand clutched at my arm, and I saw how bony and worn it had become. Losing her own baby, I thought, had left her unnaturally fearful.

I shook her off. "Don't be silly, Mama. We will both be fine." I said the words bravely, though I was suddenly filled with worry. I knew nothing about conditions on a ship.

She wrung her hands, her eyes locked on Klara, mouth working as though she would protest more. But it seemed she found no more words to say.

"Well then. God keep you, Mama." I turned my back on my childhood home.

"Wait. You'll need help at the docks."

With bewildering speed, my mother had changed tack and was pulling on her cloak, giving orders over her shoulder to Greta and climbing into my coach.

It was true—I did need help. I had our clothes and the worn linens I had brought to my marriage in the old carpetbag I had left my parents' house with, and what few household items I had dared take tied in a bundle with the nappies. I was wearing my winter coat despite the warm weather, had Klara tied into a shawl on my hip, and the ticket and a handful of precious coins slung in a carryall around my neck. An extra pair of hands would be very welcome.

It was loud and chaotic at the docks, and I was glad to have Mama at my side helping me figure out where to go. There was a long jostling line of passengers waiting to board the American ship *SS Liberty*. Donal had told me what the ship's name meant, and it seemed to me a promise of a better life ahead. We took our place in the line, and as we shuffled slowly forward with our burdens, Klara began to squirm and complain in the tight shawl. Soon she was struggling and crying, and I was having a hard time hanging on to her.

"I'll take the baby and walk her about while you wait," Mama offered, putting the carpetbag down at my side.

I never thought twice, but handed her over gratefully. The line surged forward, I dragged my bundles and bags along, and Mama hovered nearby, dandling Klara or holding on to her little fists while she toddled about. When, sweating in my coat and gripping my ticket, I finally had my turn, I was glad Mama was not at hand to hear me give my name as Sigrid Sullivan. My ticket was stamped, and then I was sent on farther to the ship's surgeon, who looked in my throat and felt my forehead and then shooed me on to the gangplank.

"Wait, I just have to get my baby." I looked back to call to my mother and could not find her in the crowd.

"Mama!" I tried to find a higher place where I could see more easily, but I was hemmed in by the people before and behind me and the ropes funneling us toward the ship.

A man in uniform motioned me along to the ship. I shook my head. "I have to go back. My mother's holding the baby."

He looked annoyed. "Be quick," he cautioned. "They won't hold the ship."

I craned my neck, hoping against hope Mama would appear at my side. More passengers were coming up behind—how could I push my way past them with all my things? "Can I leave my things here?"

Not waiting for an answer, I dumped them at his feet and struggled back, calling loudly for my mother.

She was gone. I ran through the crowds, becoming more and more frantic, but there was no sight of her.

*She's taken Klara.* As soon as the thought came to me, I knew it was true. It was not just the fear she had expressed for the baby's safety; it was the look on her face when she took Klara in her arms. I pictured it once more in my memory, and what I saw made me sick and weak. I had been so distracted, I had only seen a fond grandmother. But there was a kind of greed—or need—in the way she'd reached for my baby. It was common for weak infants to die, as her Peder had, but common can still be cruel. Perhaps even after five children, he had left an empty place in my mother's heart.

When the ticket master came to tell me my belongings had been taken aboard and it was my last chance to embark, I began weeping so hard I could hardly make myself understood. He was sympathetic enough, but the choice before me was plain: if I wanted to sail, it had to be now.

"No, I can't! I have to get my baby! Just bring my things back."

He looked dubious. "They'll be stowed belowdecks now. You'll likely have to fill out a claim form to have them sent back on the next crossing."

I stared at him, disbelieving. How could this be happening? "I have to talk to my husband. He's working on board."

He became hard. "Listen, girl. Do you see them casting off the ropes? The ship is leaving. The only question is, will you be on it or not?"

I squeezed shut my eyes and tried to think. How could I go back to Henricksen, with all my clothes and the baby's things missing? The bedding I had taken, some cookware...if I survived the beating, he would very likely cast me out.

But to leave my Klara—it was unthinkable. Then I pictured my mother, beaming down at her granddaughter, and knew that at least she would not give her to Henricksen's care. She would raise Klara herself, and he would be content to let her. Klara would be safe. But she was mine—mine and Donal's!

A firm hand fell on my arm. "You must run, if you are to board."

I sucked in a breath. I thought of Donal and America and the plans we had made. I thought of Henricksen, and the grim, dark future Klara and I both faced with him.

And, God help me, I ran up the gangplank.

## LUCY

There was more—about her misery during the crossing, their struggles to get established in Boston and the happiness she found with Donal and their other children. But I wasn't ready to read any of that. I couldn't stop thinking about Klara, about how she had had not one, but *two* chances for a decent life, and lost them both. What had killed the grandmother, I wondered, and led the grandfather to dump the baby at her stepfather's door? Was he just not able to manage with so many children and his wife gone, or had he always rejected her—the illegitimate child of his scandalous daughter?

I flipped idly through the rest of the pages, not really reading, until my eyes fell on these words on the last page:

*I wish to God I could let my daughter know that I loved her. I have prayed every day of my life that she was happy in my parents' home, as I was, and that she found a loving husband, as I did. Losing her has been my constant, secret sorrow.*

I was bawling now—and just about asphyxiating from trying to do it silently. If my mom woke up she would think I was crying for Grampa, which would make a lot more sense than falling to pieces over a little girl who lived two centuries ago. Though, now that I thought of it, maybe I *was* crying for Grampa, and my dad, and every lonely, scared, sad thing I could ever remember. I had a good long cry with two hotel pillows mashed over my head, and then I tiptoed into the bathroom, washed my face and texted Jack. **Miss you so much. Klara's story is the saddest ever. Wish you were here right now!**

# TWENTY-THREE

## KLARA

I am so lonely, I feel I will go mad with it. How have I stood here all these years, never even noticing how alone I am?

I thought of my mother earlier today, and such a wave of anguish shuddered through me that I found myself sobbing and gasping as though she was being torn out of my hands that very moment. But she was never torn; she left of her own accord. I see now, in a way I never did in life, that it was my father she was fleeing. But she left me behind, and with a man she knew would not care for me. I hate her.

Jack must come and stay with me. I *will* have someone of my own, someone who won't leave me. Not ever.

# TWENTY-FOUR

## JACK

Lucy and I were so amazed and excited about stumbling on the real Match Girl and her story that we almost forgot why we had been looking for it in the first place. I mean, not really, but we felt for a while as though finding the answer to this little mystery had actually solved the problem. We just floated around in this little oh-my-god-what-an-incredible-discovery bubble.

And I felt normal again—just having Lucy around lifted my spirits and blew away the creepy cobwebs. But between being sick and her trip to Ottawa, she was even farther behind at school than I was, so our playtime was rationed. We made a pact that we could have home-work dates as long as we actually got something done, and we more or less stuck to our vows.

A good week went by before reality reasserted itself. The reality was, we were no closer than before to knowing what to do about my little problem. And the next full moon was less than two weeks away.

The "stretched" feeling, when it came back, was almost imperceptible. If I thought about it, I felt it. If my mind was on something else, I didn't notice it. With something like this, it's a reasonable bet that thinking about it is what's making you feel that way, so I just tried to keep busy with other things. I didn't want to mess up Lucy's work— I knew how important it was to her to get through high school with no other screwups—so I didn't say anything at first. But as the moon waxed, it became harder and harder to ignore, like a noose slowly tightening around my neck.

Finally, with the full moon only a week away, I spoke up.

Her mom was in Ottawa for the weekend, sorting things out with her grandfather's house, so we had the place to ourselves and were taking full advantage. I had just discovered the tattoo on her left shoulder blade, a very kissable intertwined pattern she called a Celtic knot, when my mood suddenly changed. "Hey, Lucy."

She pulled away from me, responding to the serious tone of my voice, and I mentally kicked myself for stupid timing. Why I decided to blurt it out in the middle of our most intense make-out session ever, I'll never know. Lowered inhibition? I could tell by the expectation in her face that she thought I wanted to talk about sleeping together. Which I did—or would have back when being kidnapped by a ghost wasn't derailing the normal course of my life.

I smoothed her hair—not that Lucy's hair ever really "smoothed"—trying to cool things down a little. "Sorry. This is not…it's just—do you think you might be up for doing that spell-breaking thing again?"

She stared at me kind of blankly—I could almost see her brain shifting gears, reorienting—and then the realization that had caught up with me a week back washed over her.

"Oh God. She's still out there, still waiting for you. Of course she is. What the hell are we doing?"

She rummaged around, doing up her bra, untangling her legs from mine. By the time she sat herself straight on the edge of the bed and looked at me, she was all business.

"I'm sorry, Jack, I don't know how I—"

"It's not your fault," I cut in. "It happened to me too. I zoned out somehow. But I've been feeling really weird the last few days, too weird to ignore. And I can't think of anything else to do."

"I'll need a few minutes to get everything together," she said, and off she went. It wasn't long before I found myself cross-legged at the coffee table again, holding Lucy's hand and staring at the candle flame.

I felt a little better when it was done, but I didn't notice a dramatic release like the time before. More like the noose was loosened but not cut.

The "plan" we devised for the days leading up to the full moon was feeble, but it was all we had.

"It seems like when this happens, you're always in a sort of blanked-out, daydreamy state," said Lucy.

"I was doing math when it first happened," I protested.

"Oh. Well, were you zoning out a bit?"

"I dunno. Maybe."

"At any rate, you're more vulnerable to it when you're daydreaming—yes?"

"Yes." That much was clear.

"So can you spend the next four days being really focused and active?"

I barked out a laugh that must have sounded as frustrated and helpless as I felt, because she immediately backtracked. "Right. Sorry. That was dumb."

Still, I did end up with a little list of precautions: no booze, no dope, no posing for drawings, no gazing up at the stars, no lying in bed listening to music. No video games unless with a friend—too hypnotic.

"What about sleeping?" A bleak question. Short of an amphetamine overdose, how could I possibly keep myself awake for four nights?

Lucy considered. "Has it ever happened while you're sleeping?"

I shook my head.

"Then you're at least as safe, if not safer, sleeping than wandering around in a sleep-deprived daze," she said.

The night before the full moon, and again the night of, we repeated the spell-breaking ritual. I didn't feel any dramatic effects, but it was worth it just for the way Lucy's hand felt in mine—like a strong anchor. After two days on high alert, not sleeping well and fighting that stretched, drawn-out feeling, I began to breathe a little easier. The moon was on the wane, and so far I'd managed to stay put. Maybe the spell had worked, or the Match Girl had moved on. Maybe it would be all right.

Wrong.

~❦~

"Noah! Let's go! We were supposed to be on the road ten minutes ago." My dad's voice came booming up the stairs and into my brain.

I groaned and mashed the pillow over my ears, intent on going back to sleep.

Sunday morning. My parents didn't go to church, but they had retained some remnant idea that Sunday morning was special—meaning, in our case, a lazy interlude when kids can sleep in unmolested and parents can sit around drinking coffee and reading the paper for as long as they want. Hockey had changed all that.

I remembered now that Noah had a tournament, and my parents were driving him, plus some other kids, an hour and a half out of town to get there. Then I remembered why lying around dozing in bed might not be such a good idea. I groaned again and heaved myself out of the warm covers.

I got downstairs in time to blearily wave them off. Mom, I noticed, had armed herself with her knitting bag. I smirked into my coffee mug. She was determined to support Noah in his "passions," but she just did not get hockey. So while the other parents were glued to the game, yelling and cheering, she would be hunched into her parka, peering at her knitting needles. It was better, I guessed, than having one of those psychotic screamer parents, but likely a little embarrassing all the same.

The day yawned before me. Lucy had a shift at the café and then was having dinner out with her mom. It was Alice's birthday in a few days, but since she worked most nights, they'd decided to celebrate on her day off. "*I feel bad leaving you on your own all day,*" Lucy had said. "*It's just… she seems to really want to have a nice dinner with me, and I don't want to lose the ground we gained in Ottawa.*"

"*Geez, you don't have to apologize.*" I still couldn't quite get my head around a family in which a birthday dinner wasn't completely expected. "*Anyway, my parents and Noah will be back early this evening. And the moon is waning—I really feel like we're over the hump. I'll be fine.*"

Still, I planned to be damn careful. I laid out my day like a drill sergeant: breakfast, shower (not too long), dog walk. I cleaned out the rat cage and let the girls run around in my room. I did homework, had lunch and did the dishes Mom had asked me to take care of. Another walk and a wander through Facebook. But a focused wander, I reminded myself.

It was midafternoon when I realized I was feeling really sluggish—all I really wanted to do was take a nap. I checked my sugar, and sure enough, it had zoomed up into the low 20s. *Ugh.* I should have been well down from lunch by now. Had I forgotten my lunch insulin? I checked my pump history—no, there it was. My infusion set was only a day old and should still be fine, but I took a correction dose by injection just to be safe.

The urge to lie down and veg out was strong, as if I'd been high all day rather than just since lunch. I got myself a big bottle of water, sat myself on the couch with my computer and loaded up Netflix, searching for something exciting enough that it would keep me from spacing out. Reruns of *The Walking Dead?* Good enough.

~~~

I came to with a start, my heart pounding. *Oh no, have I...?* It was okay though; I was still in the real world. Or, on second thought, maybe not so okay—I really did feel like shit. I pulled out my meter.

Twenty-eight. What the hell? All that insulin, and I was going up—way up—not down. I padded to the bathroom, peed about a quart, drank more water and took another shot from a fresh vial of insulin. Then I changed my set for good measure, and after that there was nothing to do but wait.

I couldn't find any reason for this weird spike. But whatever—I'd had stubborn highs before. In the end it came down to math and chemistry: a big enough load of insulin *will* eventually bring down your blood sugar. The main danger was that once it started dropping, it could go really fast and send me low. So I got myself a can of Coke to have on hand, just in case, and went back to Rick Grimes and his crew.

## LUCY

Mom picked me up after work, and we went to a new Thai restaurant. "I fancy something they never serve at work," she explained. After we ordered, I slipped her the present I'd picked up at the silversmith shop next to the café.

"Sorry it's not wrapped," I said. "I only got it today." What I wanted to say, but didn't, was: *Sorry I completely ignored your birthday the year Dad died, and only managed a crappy drugstore card in the years since.*

But she was shaking her head over the silver hoops. "Lucy, they're beautiful—I love them. Thank you."

"I'll make you a cake on your real birthday."

Last year—or even a few months back—if either of us had said that, the other would have automatically dished back something along the lines of, *You don't need to bother.* Instead, my mom asked, "Stay up and eat it with me after work?"

"It's a date."

We grinned at each other, and then her eyes got all teary and, like it was contagious, mine did too. Something had definitely gotten into us lately, and in my spookier moments (which were a lot more frequent than they used to be), I suspected that *something* was my Grampa Shamus.

"God, what a couple of sucks." I dabbed at my eyes as the waiter arrived with my iced tea and my mom's wine. Her big splurge on her birthday was ordering one glass of the fancier wine instead of the cheap house wine. While we waited for our food, I showed her the special acid-free folder I'd picked up at Michael's during my work break, with Sigrid's homemade book safely protected inside. I'd been worried about crumpling or damaging it, so I was glad to have a rigid case to keep it in.

Once we'd made some inroads into the food, Mom got really serious.

"There were some things I was hoping we could talk about tonight."

"Okay…" My hackles rose, just a bit, an echo of my old What-now-leave-me-alone defensive reaction, but I took a breath and smoothed them down. We had a chance to get past that, and I didn't want to screw it up.

"First, I want to say I'm sorry." She raised a hand to head off my protest. "No, let me say it. I've left you to grow up pretty much on your own these last few years, and I am truly sorry for that. And now here you are, almost ready to fly, and no way for me to go back and do it over. But Lucy, I want you to know too that I'm so proud of you. I know you've had a hard road."

Okay, and now the tears were back. I looked at the Chiang Mai noodles hanging off my chopsticks and decided they would have to wait.

"I'm sorry too." My throat seemed determined not to let me speak, so I stopped there and reached for the iced tea. It seemed enough anyway; my mom gave me a shaky smile and managed a couple more bites before plowing on.

"So, in other news, Renata, who is on the front desk for the day shift, is quitting. She and her husband are moving out west."

Something in her voice told me this wasn't just small talk. She cleared her throat.

"I was thinking I'd ask to take over her shift."

Wow. I tried to picture what a big change that would be in our lives—my mother home when I got back after school, there for dinner, there through the evening.

"Really? I thought you didn't like those early mornings."

"I didn't. But I feel like I'm sleeping better lately. And, more important, I feel like it's time I rejoined the world—like I *want* to. You know, have a life, maybe go to a book club or a fitness class, see my friends sometimes.

"But Lucy, will it drive you crazy having me around all the time? I do want to see more of you, see if we can be a real family again. I just worry that…I know you're almost eighteen, that I can't suddenly pick up where I left off three years ago—"

"Okay, stop," I said. "I know what you're saying, and it's nice of you to ask. But if you want this job, you should definitely take it. Maybe it *will* drive me crazy sometimes. But I think it will mostly be good. Anyway, don't worry—I won't be shy about reminding you that I'm not fifteen anymore."

"No." She laughed. "No, I guess I can count on you for that."

"Well then." I held up my glass, and we clinked. "Here's to a day job," I said.

It wasn't until Mom asked me how things were going with Jack that I realized he still hadn't returned my message. He hadn't answered when I'd phoned after work, so I'd texted him a quick **everything okay?** I didn't want to panic—there were lots of reasons not to answer your phone—but I was also pretty sure he'd make a point of reassuring me as soon as he could.

"Actually, I'm a bit worried about him. He…he wasn't feeling well today, and his phone's off. Maybe you could drop me there on the way home?" I hated to lie to her when things were going so well between us, but it was the only realistic option.

I begged off dessert, saying I'd save it for a big birthday-cake pig-out. I had a bad feeling about Jack, and it was growing stronger by the minute.

# TWENTY-FIVE

## LUCY

We arrived to find an ambulance in front of the house and the door wide open. Before I jumped out of the car, I told Mom to go home, that I'd call, and then I ran into the house. The living room was so crowded with people I could hardly get a glimpse of Jack. When I did, I got really scared. He was so pale, kind of gray, and he was breathing weird, like he couldn't get enough air. Worst of all, he wasn't conscious.

One medic was fiddling with his arm, and another was holding a bag of IV solution. "How much insulin did you give him?" he asked Bente. She was standing there with one of Jack's injection pens in her hand, and she answered clearly enough, but she and Jack's dad both looked shattered.

"Ten units," she said. "That should bring him down twenty points, except it'll take more when he's this high. I didn't want to give too much because I thought the IV insulin would work much faster..." She trailed off, her voice starting to quaver like she was afraid she had done something wrong.

"That's good," the medic reassured her. "Okay, here we go, he's set up. What did you say his reading was?"

"It was off the meter," Jack's dad answered. "Just said *HI*."

"Friendly little devices, aren't they?" said the other medic, and Jack's parents tried to smile at the lame joke.

And then they were lifting Jack onto a stretcher and heading out the door—everyone was—and Jack's mom noticed me, and when I asked what happened, she said, "We found him like this—we're just back from Noah's tournament. His blood sugar's so high he's in a coma. But I can't understand how it happened so fast..."

"Will he be okay?" I blurted.

She looked at me, trying to stay calm, but her eyes were haunted. "I hope so. I'm sorry, Lucy—we've got to go with him."

"Of course," I said, and then they were gone. I stayed and wandered around the room, worrying. I didn't really know what it meant, to be in a diabetic coma, but I knew by the look on everyone's faces that it had to be serious.

I sat on the couch—still warm from Jack—and started to cry. I wanted Jack to be okay so badly, like I might die myself if he wasn't. I know that's stupid, but it's how I felt. And the worst of it was, I *knew* he wasn't okay.

Jack was in really big trouble, bigger than whatever medical emergency was going on. I knew it in my bones, knew that somehow his condition was tangled up with the creepy little Match Girl who kept pulling him into her lonely, dead world. Jack needed more than insulin, but I didn't have the first idea how to help him. I didn't even know how to get to where he was. 'Cause he wasn't at the hospital, whatever the doctors thought.

## JACK

Don't panic—it will just shoot you higher. *This is the helpful advice my mind dispenses when I find myself on Creep Street. In my opinion, panic is entirely appropriate. Everything is wrong here. I feel sicker—a lot sicker, as if even the insulin I've already injected is no longer in my body. And I'm stuck here, stuck in a way I never was before. I don't even know how I know this, except that I feel so different, as if thick rubber bands were tightening against me and pressing me against this world. I try, experimentally, to turn around and walk backward, away from the Match Girl, and am not the slightest bit surprised to find that I can't. So I walk toward her, giving in to the rubber bands, because it's that or just give up now.*

*"Jack!" Her smile makes me shudder. She seemed so help-less and innocent when I first met her. Now the look she*

trains on me is triumphant, predatory. I hold up my hand to cut her off. It's trembling so hard I have to lower it to keep from freaking myself out.

"I'm sorry, but I have to go back home right away. Please."

"Why? Because of your friends?" She spits out the question in a snarl, then takes a closer look at me. "Are you ill?"

"Yes, this time I am *ill*." Getting ill-er by the minute, in fact. The need to sit down—no, lie down—is almost too strong to fight. And I can't seem to get enough air. I heave a deep breath, knowing this too is a bad sign, that I'm burning ketones now, and that without insulin I'm heading toward a coma.

"Listen, Match Girl." I'm trying hard to connect with her, to say the right thing, but I can hardly think beyond the crisis in my body. "I know you must be lonely here, and that you've been happy to have my visits." This earns a hopeful little smile. "But I can't stay here with you. I have a disease, an illness, that needs a medicine that doesn't exist here. Without that medicine, I'll die. And I need it right now, very badly." I risk eye contact, to see if she's following me. She is, but I don't read sympathy in her expression. "If you care about me, you'll save my life and let me go."

But she's shaking her head. "No, no, Jack, I'm afraid I can't do that. I am sorry you aren't well, and I hope you won't suffer much, but don't you see? It just proves that you were sent here to be with me. If you die, then it will be even easier to stay together. We can be friends forever. You and me and my little Jack doll." She shows me a couple of tied-together sticks draped in my Kleenex, as proudly as if it were a real baby.

The lethargy creeping over me makes it hard to think. It's like my will and resolve are draining away with my energy. Just lie down and rest, *my body croons to me*. Close your eyes for a while; that will feel so-o-o-o much better. *I force myself to focus, to ignore my weird breathing, the ugly ketone taste in my mouth, the rising nausea, and keep arguing with her. Begging, really, is what it amounts to, and it's getting me nowhere, but what else can I do?*

*What finally overcomes me is the desperate need to pee.* "I need to—" *I gesture toward my crotch.*

"Just go in one of the buildings," *she says*. "There's no one to see you."

*I heave open a door, step into an empty room—is it a room? I have strong doubts that a back wall exists beyond the shadows—and unzip. A bucket of urine pours out—my body's feeble attempt to get rid of the extra sugar coursing through it—and on its heels comes a lost-in-the-Sahara thirst. I know without asking, there is no water here. And with that my resolve fails. Slowly, one hand against the wall for support, I make my way to the other side of the door. I let my legs fold under me, and I curl up in the corner. Lying down has never been such a relief. My eyes snap open with a surge of fear when I recall the little doll, the Match Girl's hairs wrapped tightly around the matchstick figure. I imagine I can feel those hairs like cables coiled around my own neck. Why didn't I grab the doll and smash it, peel the hairs away? I try to make myself get up and do it now— but I can't. I'm sinking, black water closing over me, going, going, gone.*

## LUCY

I'm making it up as I go along, pulling from a random assortment of witch movies, YouTube yoga lessons and the kooky stuff I read on the Internet while researching spells. I'm trying to induce an altered state, to let go of my conscious brain so my mind can slip away. It feels completely impossible with my heart racing from anxiety and my head so full of worry. Plus, I have a growing sense of urgency that is fighting my attempts to relax at every turn. *He's dying!* it screams at me. *Quit pissing around— you'll be too late!*

Still, I make Jack's room as dark as I can, sit in front of the candle I lifted from the fireplace mantel, do my calming yoga breaths and try to focus on my breath going in and out, on the candle's wavering light, on a state of peace. I try to float, to let my mind be still, to accept what comes to it.

Twice I lose it, swearing and beating the ground in frustration that I'm so helpless and scared, that pretending to be some sort of mystic is the best I can come up with. But it *is* the best I can come up with, so I make myself go back and try again, and this time I think about the

Match Girl. In fact, after a couple of minutes I get my bag and pull out the folder with her mother's story in it. I take out the old pages and hold them close.

Little Klara. Her story haunted me when I was little. My mom read it to me by mistake, I think—we found the collection of fairy tales at a yard sale, and she bought it for me because I loved the full-page color illustrations. I remember that when she got close to the end, she kind of stopped and said, "*Oh. This isn't a very happy story. Let's try the next one.*" But I was already hooked—the Match Girl was so young, like me, and so obedient (not like me) and so cold—and I made her finish it. And then, of course, I had nightmares for days afterward. The next year I learned to read, and I read that story over and over, crying over her sad fate. I know, I know, she was all happy in heaven, but I only thought about her blue, stiff body and her brute of a father.

And now it turns out that Klara is my relative. And her real story is even sadder than the book, so sad my heart breaks for the little girl and young mother pulled apart against their will.

*And then I'm there—oh my god, I'm there, right on the street Jack described, and it's just like he said—the sooty buildings, the mist, the damp cobblestones. Jack said he felt strangely calm when he first went there, but I don't. I'm freaking out, because, I realize, a part of me never actually believed in this place. I'm all racy with adrenaline, my heart hammering so fast they might need to call an ambulance for me next.*

*She's standing there, just like in the story, so frail and wispy-looking, her clothes worn thin and frayed. I walk up to her, willing my legs to move forward, trying to order them to stop shaking, and she trains her big blue eyes on me, and I can actually feel the hairs on the back of my neck—which I didn't even realize I had—stand up. The spiders are crawling again, up and down my spine, as we size each other up.*

*She looks like me, I think, and that's what sets the spiders off. It's the eyes, I guess, and the shape of her face—she looks like my half-starved Victorian little sister.*

*I expect her to ask me to buy some matches, but she doesn't. Instead, her eyes narrow and her pinched little face tightens up even smaller.*

*"What are you doing here?" is what she says, and not politely either.*

*What am I supposed to do? Beat her up? She's dead already (and oh boy, does that send the spiders racing). I doubt I could even hurt her. Threaten her? With what? Grab Jack and run? Where would we go?*

*I can't think what to say, so I'm just standing there like an idiot, staring at her, and I think again about the shitty little life she had, cut off so soon, and now here she is, stuck in some ghastly movie-set world all by herself, and I just feel sorry for her. It's really weird, how I can feel frantic for Jack and sorry for Klara all at the same time. And I think maybe my only chance, however faint, is to try to befriend her.*

*I say the first thing that comes into my head.*

"Hello, Klara. I've wanted to help you ever since I was a little girl." And it's true. I did used to wish I could help her—bring her inside, warm her up and feed her, make her my little sister. I remember that now.

She looks at me like I'm crazy, shakes her head and says in her thin little voice, "No. You're just saying that to get to Jack."

Smart cookie.

"It's true that I'd like to see Jack," I say carefully. "But it's also true that your story made me really sad when I was young. I'm not lying about that."

Her big blue eyes probe me, but she doesn't say anything, so I venture on.

"Is Jack here, Klara?"

"Yes, he's back there." She motions vaguely toward a stained brick building with an arched doorway. "He'll be dead soon, I expect." She lights up in a smile that is pretty much the scariest thing I ever saw. "Then we can be together for real."

Oh no. Oh, Jack, hang on. Little Klara is crazy, and I'm so far out of my league it's not funny.

"Please, Klara" is the most I can manage, and she turns on me.

"Why do you keep calling me that?" Her gaze intent, almost ferocious.

I take a step backward without meaning to, as if she might start shooting laser beams out of her dead eyes.

"Isn't that your name? And your mother was Sigrid."

*Oh, that gets her attention. She's like a feral cat on high alert.*

*"We're related, you know. I'm Lucy. Klara, Lucy— we both have a name that means 'light.'" Am I babbling? I make myself stop and watch her reaction.*

*"Klara." She tries it on, softly. "Klara."*

*"Don't you know your name?" I ask.*

*"I didn't think I had one." Then her eyes snap back to me. She's not the vague, floaty creature I saw over the river. Not at all. She's focused, and Christ, she sure seems alive. "How do you know anything about it? You weren't even born then."*

*"I found your mother's notebook. It tells her whole story—the real story." In fact, I'm still clutching it against my chest—until this moment I hadn't even noticed that it came with me. I hold it out to show her.*

*"My mother abandoned me." Her little reedy voice hard and scornful, covering up the hurt. Oh, I know that voice. "I don't care anything about her."*

*"Oh, Klara, is that what he told you? It's not true. She loved you."*

*Her shoulders hunch up, so scrawny but doing their best to protect her. "No. If she loved me, she wouldn't have left me."*

*"She didn't. She tried to take you with her. She was going to America, to start a new life with you and your real father. He loved you too. He loved both of you." Her eyes are trained on me now, big and blue and dangerous. I realize that if she decides I'm lying about something so important, about the biggest pain of her painful life, she'll kill me along*

with Jack. *The spiders are everywhere, the effort not to panic making me shake all over. I force myself to meet those spooky eyes. "She was tricked, Klara. Your grandmother came to the docks to help her, but then she ran off with you as Sigrid was boarding. Your mother couldn't find you, and she couldn't go back. She was heartbroken over it. And then your grandmother died, so you were sent back to your...to Henricksen."*

*"Is that what she wrote—in there?" She gestures to the notebook but makes no move to take it.*

*I nod. "Everything that happened is in here."*

*Klara's face closes down, and she shakes her head. "And I'm to believe someone like her could read and write?" Her voice is scornful, but I can see the emotional struggle playing out on her features, and I know—at least, I hope I know, because if I'm reading her wrong things could go very bad very quickly—that she* wants *to believe me. Wants it desperately. She may have grabbed on to Jack as a kind of consolation prize, but what she yearned for through her whole short life was her mother.*

*"She didn't write this herself," I explain. "She got someone to write it down for her." Daughter-in-law, I almost said, and realized just in time that Klara might not take kindly to the idea of other children.*

*"Read it then."*

*"What?" A pathetic stall. I heard her, all right.*

*"Read it. If this is the whole story that my mother wanted me to know, then read it to me." She crosses her thin arms across her chest and glares at me.*

"There isn't time, Klara," I plead. "Jack is in a really a bad way. He needs help fast, and this is long—it took me two nights to read it."

Her chin lifts in defiant stubbornness, and, oh God, I recognize the gesture. I do it myself when I need to hang tough. "Read the important parts then. Read it, and then I'll decide if what you've brought is worth giving up Jack."

There's nothing for it but to read. Hang on, Jack, I think, and then I open the notebook and flip to the place where Sigrid is forced to marry. I scan the page, then begin: "Sit down, Sigrid, your father has news." I read up to the scene with the priest, skip some pages and pick it up at "Klara is my only joy, but I worry after her as well." I read the scene where Donal arrives, and then I jump to the docks where Klara is taken. One part of my mind is screaming at how long this is taking, but I know I have to give her enough to make it real. I don't dare steal a glance at her until I come to a stop, where Sigrid boards the ship.

Klara's blue eyes are blurred with tears. Her face crumples and then so do her legs, until she's huddled on the pavement, rocking herself back and forth. I have one last card to play.

"Klara…she left a message for you."

"For me?" She seems shocked, as if she can't conceive of anyone leaving anything for her. I nod. "Tell me."

I hesitate. "Let me see Jack first."

She jumps to her feet, eyes blazing. "TELL me!"

I stand my ground. "I need to see Jack."

*She flicks her hand impatiently, as if swatting away a fly. "Jack will be fine for another minute. You can see him after."*

*I don't have time to play chicken. I turn to the last page and force myself to read slowly and clearly,* "I wish to God I could let my daughter know that I loved her. I have prayed every day of my life that she was happy in my parents' home, as I was, and that she found a loving husband, as I did. Losing her has been my constant, secret sorrow."

*"She said that?"*

*I just nod. Scared as I am, and frantic to see Jack, I can't help but be moved by Klara's response. Like this big poisoned well of hurt and hate is draining out of her. When she finally speaks, she is wistful, tentative, like she's almost afraid to say it.*

*"Do you think...do you think if I went with the other dead people, she'd be there? Would she want to see me?"*

*Oh God. What do I know about ghosts and heaven and the afterlife? I'm tempted to paint it up as pretty as possible, to say anything to take her mind off Jack. But somehow I know it's important not to lie—that she'll know if I lie to her.*

*"I don't know where people go after they die, Klara. But I do know that if your mother is there, she will want to wrap her arms around you and hold you close."*

*She smiles at this, the most wistful, sweet smile.*

*"You can have the book, Klara. It's yours, from your mother." I hold it out, and this time she takes it. And I take my chance. "Can I see Jack now? You said I could."*

*She points without lifting her eyes from the book, like she's not even thinking about Jack anymore. "Through that doorway."*

# TWENTY-SIX

## LUCY

*I yank open the heavy door and rush in. It's so dark inside, I don't see him at first. He's curled in a ball in the corner. I yell at him, grab his hand, smack his face, but his eyelids don't even flutter. How can I get him out of here if he won't wake up?*

*The door opens, and I jump up. I don't want my back turned to Klara, sisterly fantasies or no. But she just sticks her head in the door.*

*"You may as well have this. It's of no use to me anymore." She tosses something at me. It skitters a few inches across the floor like an ungainly insect. Her stick man of Jack. "I took the hair off."*

*And she's gone. I don't know what she means about the hair, but I take the doll. Should I break it? I decide it's Jack's,*

not mine, and I stick it inside his plaid shirt. I get kind of
frantic about tying the ends of the shirt so it stays in, and so
I don't notice at first that Jack is stirring.

"Lucy?" The words are slurred but there.

"Jack! Oh, thank God, Jack!" Relief makes me weak and
giddy, though I know we aren't out of the woods yet. "Can
you sit up?" I slide my arm under him and try to help while
he props himself against the wall.

"Oh, man. I feel like crap." I can see memory returning
to him, and with it, panic. "We have to get out of here.
We have to—"

"I know." I hold both of his hands, try to hold his eyes
with my own. "I think she'll let you go now. Let's just see if
you can walk."

Walking is a tall order. Jack can hardly stay awake. But
he can crawl— just—so that's what we do. I stand up to
open the door, and then I crawl beside him, trying to make
sure he doesn't suddenly land on his face.

The Match Girl—Klara—is not in her usual spot. I scan
quickly and spot her across the street. She's walking slowly
toward an alley, an alley swirling with mist that no longer
looks sooty and sinister. It's shot with pearly light and hints
of rose and gold, and I find myself wishing, just a bit, that I
could go with her.

"Klara!" I call. Jack looks at me like I'm crazy, but...
she's my sister.

She glances over her shoulder, a little impatient.

"I hope you find her," I say. "You deserve to be happy."

*She nods, a solemn acknowledgment, and gives me a little wave that makes her seem like a child again. And she steps into the mist.*

"Okay, off we go, Jack. Just a little farther, love."

*Jack toils down the street, stopping every few feet to rest. If we aren't home by the time we reach the end, I don't think we'll get home at all.*

*Home. Oh geez.* "Jack, you're not at home!"

"Wha'?" *He's barely able to speak, maybe not able to comprehend. It's taking everything he's got just to keep moving.*

"You're at the hospital. It might be important to know that." *Who knows how it works? What if his…whatever we are now goes back to his living room and his body's not there?*

And then everything goes black, and I'm sitting cross-legged in Jack's bedroom in front of a burned-out candle, stiff and chilly but definitely back on Earth.

## JACK

I heard the voices first.

"C'mon, Bente, it's only been a few minutes since the last test."

"I know, but Guy, why isn't it coming down? They're pouring insulin right into his veins, and it's not budging."

"I know. I don't know."

They sounded beyond worried, really scared, and even though I wanted to just rest for a while and wallow in the relief that I wasn't dead, I had to let them know I was okay. I pried my eyes open and squinted against the glare of hospital fluorescents. Obnoxious modern lighting had never looked so good. I tried out my voice.

"Hey..."

You'd think *I* was the ghost, the way they stared at me. Then my mother burst into tears and threw herself on me; my dad, with a sound like he'd had the wind knocked out of him, grabbed my hand in both of his and then actually kissed it.

"Guy, get the nurse!" My mom was fumbling with my meter, fitting in a new strip and extracting my hand from Dad's paw.

"Let me," I said. "You suck at it." Her laugh was halfway to a sob, but I could tell she felt a bit reassured. I was still shaky, and in the end she had to steady my hand as I applied the strip. She gasped when she saw the result.

"Twenty-two? You were still off the scale ten minutes ago!"

Five minutes later, Dad returned with a nurse in tow. She pulled out her industrial-grade meter—the kind with lancets that feel like paper punches—and drilled a hole in my finger.

"18.3." We stared at each other as the new worry surfaced.

"He's dropping too fast. He needs—"

"Glucose." The nurse cut my mom off briskly. "The doctor left standing orders." She was fiddling with my

IV leads as she spoke, taking away one bag, replacing it with another. "No more insulin for you, young man. And welcome to the land of the living."

After she left, a hush descended, like we didn't know where to begin. Finally, my mom couldn't wait any longer.

"Jack, what hap—"

"Shh, Bente." My dad walked over and put his arm around her. "Let the boy get back on his feet first." He reached over and grabbed my hand again. "But you scared the very piss out of us, Jack, and that's the truth."

"I know. Me too." Soon I would have to decide what to tell them, but for now I had a reprieve. I didn't want to even think about the inquisition that would follow with my new doctor. God, I could picture it now: the lecture on taking responsibility, the social worker asking earnestly if I had made a "cry for help." I lay back and closed my eyes—and as memory sharpened, anxiety clenched my gut.

"Where's Lucy?" I bolted up in the bed. *What if she didn't make it?* "Did she get home?"

Mom looked guilty. "We left her at the house. I should have checked in with her." Her hand shot up to her mouth. "And Noah! Is he still at the team party? What time is it?"

"I'll call him." Dad was dialing when a new nurse showed up at the door. She frowned at me.

"There a young woman at the desk who wants to see you. She says her name is—"

"Lucy." Lucy looked worn out but hadn't lost any of her attitude. She ducked around the nurse and launched herself at me. More tears. Finally we let go, and she took a good look at me. "Not awesome, but a lot better than last time I saw you."

And we both knew where *that* had been. I pulled her back into another hug and whispered in her ear, "Thank you. Thank you for coming after me." I was full of questions about how she'd managed it, but they would have to wait.

# TWENTY-SEVEN

## JACK

"So…what're your plans for the Christmas holidays?"

It was mid-December, six inches of perfect snow fresh on the ground, Christmas flyers jamming the mailbox every morning. Lucy and I were trudging back to her place; math club was back on the schedule, and we were both in a final push to catch up and be in the clear by Christmas break.

"Funny you should mention that. My mom was saying we should go to Cuba for Christmas. Courtesy of my grampa."

"Oh, sweet. Lucky you."

"Yeah, well, it turns out it will have to wait till next year. Someone at work already put in for vacation over Christmas week, and with all the stat holidays, they can't spare two."

"Oh. Boo."

"Yeah. So what are you doing?"

"I was thinking I'd go to Montreal for a few days over New Year's."

Lucy nodded. "Be nice to see your friends."

"Yeah. I was hoping you'd come with me."

"Oh." She stopped and looked up at me. It was snowing again, the kind of wet snowflakes that stick to each other on the way down and grow huge. Her red tam had collected a lacy layer of snow. "You dare introduce me to your friends?"

"I guarantee they will like you. And there will be a New Year's party for sure. But we don't have to go to it—if you'd rather, we can go out for dinner and wander around Old Montreal. There'll be something going on there."

"I've never been. That sounds great."

She threaded her arm into mine, and we kept walking, planning our little trip as we went.

Neither of us mentioned that between Christmas and New Year's there would be another full moon. I honestly wasn't worried.

The Match Girl was gone. We'd seen her go, but even if we hadn't, I think I would still have known. Through those weird months, her presence had grown on me, so that I could feel her hovering...not over me, exactly. Behind me? I didn't even realize I could feel her until I felt her absence.

It wasn't even three weeks ago that I'd almost died because of her, but it seemed so distant. Not like a dream—I knew it was real, all right—but like something that happened so long ago it was getting hard to remember. And that was fine with me.

It was different for Lucy. She had some bond with Klara that I didn't understand, more than could be explained by the discovery of some distant ancestral connection. Whatever went down between them, I think that memory will always burn bright for Lucy.

We still haven't decided what we're doing next year. I know the odds are against high-school couples staying together, but I want to try. Lucy and I are good for each other.

Besides, if there's one thing the Match Girl taught me, it's that love is not so easy to find. Some people go their whole lives without it. So of course we want to hang on to love when it comes our way.

But not so tight that we strangle each other. That's the other thing I know more about now: the destructive side of love.

By the way, I burned Little Jack in the kitchen sink. It didn't hurt a bit.

# AFTERWORD

Hans Christian Andersen did keep diaries that have been published, but the passage Jack reads in *Drawn Away* is entirely fictional. I am not aware of any evidence that Andersen's story "The Little Match Girl" was inspired by a real event or person—though it does seem possible.

Type 1 diabetes is a lifelong disease that strikes children and youth and destroys the ability of their pancreases to make insulin. Before the discovery and development of injectable insulin in the early 1920s (by Frederick Banting, in Toronto, Canada), type 1 diabetes was a certain death sentence. Today we can treat the disease, but there is still no cure.

For those curious about Jack's blood sugar, or blood glucose (BG), readings, the normal range is between 4 and 7 mmol/L (millimoles per liter). When it drops even a bit below 4, things can quickly become serious—that's why Jack always carries some kind of sugar for treating a low.

There's a much greater range of high blood sugars than low. When the meter just reads *HI*, like Jack's did, that indicates an extremely high BG of over 30. Even a very high BG is not an immediate emergency like a low is, but when it is prolonged or untreated, it can lead to coma and eventually death. The higher the BG, the sooner the situation becomes critical.

Canada, where Jack lives, uses a different system of blood-glucose measurement than the US, where the normal range is 72-126 mg/dL (milligrams per deciliter).

# ACKNOWLEDGMENTS

My thanks go out to all the people who make a book like this possible: my agent, Amy Tompkins; my insightful and patient editor, Sarah Harvey; the copyeditors, proofreaders, cover artists and designers whom I haven't met but who make my book so much better.

I also want to thank my dear friend Susan Newman for finding the perfect title and sending it my way.

Above all, I want to send out my appreciation to the kids and young adults who remain eager readers in an age when so many insist that "nobody reads anymore." Oh yes, we do!

HOLLY BENNETT is a writer and editor living in Peterborough, Ontario. The author of six young adult novels—most recently *Shapeshifter* and *Redwing*—she is inexplicably drawn to the paranormal, the fantastic and the mythic. *Drawn Away* is her first contemporary novel. For more information, visit www.hollybennett.ca.